elixir

DAVIS
BUNN

WestBow
P R E S S
A Division of Thomas Nelson Publishers
Since 1798

2335

Published by WestBow Press, a division of Thomas Nelson, Inc.

Publisher's Note: This novel is a work of fiction. Names, characters, places, and incidents are either products of the author's imagination or used fictitiously. All characters are fictional, and any similarity to people living or dead is purely coincidental.

ISBN 0-7394-4143-4

Printed in the United States of America

This book is dedicated to three friends,
wise men all

Chip MacGregor
Don Pape
Steve Arterburn

---

whose wonderful gifts of spiritual wisdom and
creative insight helped me forge this story.

TAYLOR STOOD ATOP THE CLIFF OF GUETHARY.
The hill's curved ascent formed an immense sound baffle so
that the ocean roared at him from all sides. Below him the narrow cobblestone lane snaked between red-roofed Basque houses
to the medieval harbor. Further out to sea, the cliff's natural
enclosure had been extended into great stone arms. These pro-
tective walls rose twenty feet above the ocean's surface and nar-
rowed the harbor mouth. Today the surf was so mammoth
each inside wave crashed over the walls and bathed the stone

in foam. A mist rose from the skirmish of water against rock, drifting like earthbound clouds. Taylor Knox breathed the salt-laden air and knew a piercing regret over having been brought to this magnificent realm on such an impossible quest.

A trio of doll-sized surfers began the paddle through the harbor entrance and out into the wash. The outside break was gigantic. Even from this height, Taylor knew that he was staring at the biggest waves he had ever seen. It was one thing to dream about surfing the behemoths of the Basque country. It was another thing entirely to have no excuse for not paddling out.

"Puts the old gut in a right twist, that." Kenny Dean was a Brit who had migrated from London to Devon by way of Australia's Gold Coast. "First time I caught sight of the heavies out there, I felt the old fear factor grab my throat like a noose." He clapped Taylor on the shoulder. "Cheer up, Yank. It's a lot worse than it looks."

Red Harris moved up to Taylor's other side. "I don't see how that's possible."

"Get yourself down to sea level; things will look different, believe you me." Kenny sounded vastly satisfied with the prospect. "Eyeball to eyeball, these beasties have a way of positively clearing the mind."

There were a lot of people watching, but fewer than two dozen surfers in the water. Taylor stood in a tiny park on a cliff-side promontory, surrounded by surfers from around the globe—

Japan, Brazil, Spain, Portugal, California, New Zealand, France, Australia. Knights in neoprene armor, drawn by the prospect of battling the mythical dragons in their deep blue realm.

"Time to motivate," Kenny urged. "It doesn't get better with the waiting."

The three of them suited up and started down the cobblestone lane. The alley was shadowed by the close-set Basque houses, all of them whitewashed and asymmetrical. The Basque considered their village architecture a gesture of both unity and defiance. The bright red roofs shone in the sunlight like brilliant steps clambering up the Pyrenees cliffside.

They rounded the final corner and halted. The blue sky and light offshore wind were mocked by rumbling thunder. All the gaily colored Basque fishing boats were in harbor today. Late August and early September marked the first of the big Arctic howlers, lows deeper than hurricane eyes and storms broad as Greenland. Two thousand miles north, a tempest was sending out waterborne mountains. For the past three days, as Taylor and his traveling buddies had made their way south from the Normandy ferry port, all the French surf shops and surfers' hostels had meteorological charts tacked to their front doors. Forget the tourist brochures and their photos of placid Riviera waters. This was France's other face. The Basque locals still called the Bay of Biscay by its medieval name, the Bone Coast.

The water was jewellike beyond the harbor walls, flattening

between sets until the sea became a vivid reflection of the sky's brilliant blue. Then the next set stacked up like liquid corduroy, and the first wave struck the harbor walls. The sound of water upon stone was a great booming wrath. The wash drenched the stone in white, then retreated. The boats were tucked up tight against the cliff walls, as far from the harbor mouth as possible. Even so, they rocked like bathtub toys.

And this was the *inside* wave.

The next wave hissed over the rock beach as Taylor launched himself into the sea. The retracting wave sucked him out fast. By his third stroke he was already halfway to the harbor mouth. The barrier rocks were big as cars, the stone arms they formed thirty feet thick. When the next breaking wave poured across in foamy whitewash, Taylor felt the thunder in his chest. The retreating wave drew him out and through the wall and into the inside break.

Once through the harbor entrance, Taylor passed into a deep-water channel. He had never paddled so hard in his life. The central channel remained calm, save for miniature whirlpools spun by the crashing waves. To either side, the furious torrent boomed over the harbor rocks.

Taylor pulled over the last of the set waves and entered a calm interlude. The sea mocked him with placid serenity, impersonal in its power. Taylor's two companions drew up to either side, puffing from both the paddle and the realm they had entered.

Ahead, the channel broadened. Taylor could see the stream spread out like rippling underwater fingers. The tidal suction lessened, but further out the set waves formed long unbroken walls. Which meant timing for the final outside push was a matter of survival.

The world's seventh-deepest ocean basin was only twenty miles off the Basque coast. The entire coastline was shaped like cupped hands four hundred miles wide, forming the Bay of Biscay. The bay was aimed straight north, which meant that when the great Arctic storms created their mammoth surges, the Basque coast became crowned by the largest and thickest waves in the North Atlantic. From the second week in August to the last of November, seldom did a week pass without at least one day of waves over twenty feet.

The next set arrived. To either side of Taylor's deepwater perch, the inside waves jacked up twice his height. Call them twelve feet. A bodyboarder took off and screamed his way down the face, flying so fast he skipped like a Styrofoam rock over the surface. Then the wave's lip came down like a blue-crystal fist and hammered the bodyboarder into liquid oblivion.

Taylor turned shoreward. The harbor mouth looked miniscule from here. He could actually see the wash suck through, a great hush of water. The only way in was to face the lineup, catch a wave, and surf it away from the port. To the north, a hardscrabble beach formed the only safe exit. As another set wave rose and broke to either side, Taylor watched three surfers clamber over the rocks and stumble up a path that meandered along the cliffside. He tracked further up to the cliffside park, full of watchers. Beyond them, a group of older locals stood beneath the plantain shade trees and observed both the surfers and a game of pelota.

Taylor focused on the cliffside scene and did his best to ignore the raging fury to either side. He was living a dream. Of course he was afraid. But he would not let that fear defeat him. He would ignore how the surfers stumbled in abject exhaustion as they mounted the cliffside path. He would think instead of the green and purple mountains, the golden drifting mist, the beauty of this day.

Taylor found himself recalling the lessons he had studied back in Iona. The Scottish monk's voice became intensely audible. The old man could have been seated there beside him, sharing this day of crystal blue. The monk's name was Brother Jonah, and he had known his own time in the whale's gullet, though he had never told Taylor the entire story. Only that God had been forced to seal Jonah inside his greatest fear to gain his attention. The monk was stunted and twisted like the shoreline cedars of St. Augustine, Taylor's home. But Jonah's eyes were as vivid as this day, and his voice held such gentle passion he could speak to Taylor about things Taylor had spent a lifetime ignoring. And Taylor had listened. He listened still.

When the sea quieted once more, he was ready.

The paddle from the safe channel to the outside lineup was

over a quarter of a mile. Taylor grunted deep and heavy in his chest with each downstroke. There were six of them paddling now, joined by three surfers returning from the last set.

Taylor was the first to spot the long dark line. He gave up enough breath to shout, "Incoming!"

They all accelerated. The time for holding back was gone. Taylor could hear the others panting with the effort and the fear. Eyeball to eyeball, Kenny had said. The next set was a rising dark shadow separating sea from sky. Mentally there was no room for anything more than the next deep stroke, the next breath, the next glimpse of the distance yet to cover.

In the outside lineup, two surfers peeled away and began paddling south, toward the channel. Taylor heard Red groan. He agreed with the sentiment but could not spare the breath. There was only one reason surfers in the lineup would move over. The peak, the highest portion of the wave and the first to break, was aimed for the channel. Straight at them.

The wave was so large Taylor could not tell how far he had yet to travel. It was already the largest wave he had ever seen up close, and still it was seventy-five yards away, perhaps more. Taylor's shoulder tendons popped with each stroke. The wave was sweeping grandly toward him, a mobile crag with a face so clean and pure it caught the sunlight and blinded him. Taylor squinted against the glare and began the climb up the wave's face. Up and up and up, rising so fast now his gut swooped. The wave's leading edge began to feather just as he crested the peak. To his right one of the waiting surfers paddled furiously and made it over the ledge and disappeared.

To his other side, Red crested the ledge and leaned back, panting hard as he pushed himself to a seated position.

Taylor caught sight of what lay ahead and screamed, "Don't stop!"

Beside him Kenny shouted as well, but the words were lost to the thunder and the spray from the wave crashing behind them. Ahead rose a wave larger than the first. The larger the wave, the further out it broke. They were not safe yet.

Taylor pushed beyond his limits. He had to make it over. His chest was on fire. He did not have enough air left for a long holddown. And being caught inside on a wave this size would mean a trip to the bottom. Surfers had a term for the area in front of a large wave. They called it the impact zone.

He clawed his way up the face. Blinded by the spray, he was too afraid of what might lie further on to stop. Which was good. Because the third wave was largest of all, so huge even the surfers further out were pushing for the horizon.

Midway up the third face, Taylor knew he could not make it over.

His mind in panic mode, Taylor did the only thing he knew to do. The last thing he wanted was to let go of his only flotation, his only source of steady breath. But there was still more than ten feet of face to claw up, and already the lip was shattering like glass as the wave began its inexorable descent. So he slid off his board, gripped the tail, and stabbed the board with all his might *through* the wave.

He felt the wave grip him and knew he was going over. Falling away, descending into the maelstrom of a twenty-five-foot monster. Taylor was struggling to draw a final gasping breath when the leash connecting his ankle to the board snapped taut. His board was through the wave and out the other side. At the last possible moment, it plucked him up and away to safety.

Taylor came up gasping, shaking the water from his eyes, clambering onto his board and paddling even before he could see. Then he stopped.

Ahead of him was only calm and blue and sea.

He had to lock his gut muscles to halt his trembling. To his right, a trio of locals chatted easily in French, as though it were just another day at the café. One man laughed and plowed a surfer's trail with a flat hand.

Kenny's voice sounded as shaky as Taylor felt. "Red didn't make it."

Taylor looked back. Far, far to shore, a little figure pulled himself out of the whitewash. The passing set had littered the sea with a froth so thick Red was turned hoary white, his entire body lathered with foam. But he was moving. A good sign.

Thankfully, the next set was long in coming. They sat and watched as Red paddled toward them. His arms were so weary he could scarcely raise his hands clear of the water. When he arrived, he straddled his board and sat trembling, breathing through a throat made raspy by swallowing seawater.

"All right, mate?" Kenny asked.

Red gulped a breath and managed, "Should've never stopped."

Kenny pretended not to notice the man's state. "If ever you catch a wave early in a set, best make ruddy sure to ride it far enough over to miss getting hammered by the others."

There was nothing to be gained from rushing. Taylor sat through the next set. He studied the other surfers, saw how they watched for waves coming from both the north and the north-west. He saw how the northwest sets were larger, but the right walls sectioned and often closed out, a sure trip to the impact zone. He studied the locals' takeoff positions, how they stationed themselves, the way they aimed either for the channel or the far reaches of the beachside where the inside waves lacked serious power. He read the sea as carefully as he could, drawing from an ocean-drenched life. He paddled for one wave he did not intend to take, measuring the draw up the face. The larger the wave, the more water rushed up the face, pulling the surfer off the back. Going for a big wave meant total commitment. Aggression and power and determination so focused it bordered on rage were required to make it over the ledge. Fear was a far worse killer than the wave itself.

When the next set arrived, Taylor moved for position. He was closest to the peak and thus in the spot to claim the first wave. Two of the French guys backed off when they saw him going. There was one heartstopping moment when he saw the pit for the first time, lost in shadows far below. The wave had not yet started to break, but already he could hear the bellow, or perhaps it was just his heart. His mind screamed to pull out, push away, drop to safety. Taylor yelled back, shouting so hard his voice went falsetto, using all the air in his lungs to shove the fear aside. To either side the lip began to feather. The chasm below hunched and opened, the wave ledged, and Taylor was over and falling.

The big-wave gun was twice as heavy as the surfboard he used in Florida, and as steady as a table. Taylor rose to his feet and almost tumbled when the board did not give as he was accustomed. His arms did a gull-like swing; he shifted back and steadied into proper balance. His descent was so smooth he was down below eye level before he could actually accept the fact that he had caught his first monster.

Then he screamed again.

The crashing thunder drowned out everything. This was a singular moment, one between him and the ocean and the wave. The windless water was so calm he glided as on air. He reached and touched the wave's face, trailing one hand along the wall. He drew himself closer still, leaning into the mobile force. The wave was a mountain; he was tucked inside the very depths. And he never wanted this moment to end. Never.

The wall by his face began to bow slightly. Taylor felt a visceral awareness, born of this adrenaline-drenched intimacy.

The Guethary break rarely formed the liquid tunnels called tubes. Instead the leading edge tumbled into a great freight train of noise and froth. Taylor could sense the foaming maw edge ever closer. High overhead, the wave's leading edge raced ahead in warning. He risked being shut down, trapped, hammered. Taylor crouched and drew his board up the now vertical face, adding the speed of constant descent. He remained untouched by all but the spray.

The spray. It roared out in a puffing blast, punched forward by the bellowing wave. Taylor was blinded. He shook his eyes clear. He was encased in a watery realm. Up ahead was blue sea and mirror sparkles and sunlight. Around him was a different universe entirely, one of power and speed and liquid cannonades and impossible balance. He wanted to shout, but his throat was clenched by an ecstasy as tight as real pain.

Too soon it was over. Too soon. He crouched lower and lower to maintain his flight as long as the wave would allow. Finally the wave spun him into a farewell funnel. He straightened and stood there an instant longer, hands gripping the sky and the moment. Far in the distance, other figures raised their arms and hooted. He fell into the water, wishing he could make eternal what was already gone.

TAYLOR CAUGHT A SECOND WAVE. AND A THIRD. AFTER the fourth wave, the paddle out caused stabbing pains in his shoulders and arms. When he came upright on his board and the adrenaline surge from the last wave and the race for safety diminished, his body could not shake off the water's chill. He hungered for more, but to stay out when he was growing so fatigued meant risking serious injury.

He sat through the next set, just reveling in the day. The sun caught each wave and transformed it into a peak of burnished gold. As the wave fell, the feathering lip sent back a sheet of spray that formed earthbound rainbows. The cliffside was packed now with families. Old men leaned and pointed at the breaking waves with their canes. Mothers pushed strollers; young lovers ate sorbet and took in the spectacle. It was an utterly French scene, flavored with the Basque spices of explosive nature and craggy cliffs and Monet's sunlight.

The day's final wave was the largest Taylor had ever ridden. He made long sweeping turns, flying from crest to pit and back again. He rode with his back to the face now, headed for the northern beach. When the inside segment started to form up, the entire wave crested together. A closeout was something to avoid at all costs here. He had no idea what the bottom was like, but he suspected the same boulders that littered the beach were also underwater. He flipped off the back of the wave and slipped onto his board, pointed seaward.

He came up in the eerie calm between sets. It was tempting to remain where he was and not sever the aquatic umbilical cord tying him to the day. But he knew the calm was a myth.

The ocean was not tranquil. The force was merely gathering for the next eruption. He flipped his board around and headed toward shore.

That was when Taylor saw the attacker.

Where the surfer's path jinked in its climb up the cliffside, a rock ledge jutted seaward. The shooter tried to mask himself behind a stunted pine. But the tree was too small, and the shooter's position left half his body exposed. The rifle barrel looked as big as a cannon.

The first shot ripped open the water not three feet from him. The boom rolled down just as the man pumped the bolt action.

Taylor dove hard for the bottom.

The second bullet struck his board. He heard the crack of fiberglass exploding above his head. The bottom was lost beneath a cloud of silt dislodged by the waves. He found the seabed by colliding with a rock the size of a van. Taylor grabbed a handhold and listened to three more deadly chimes plunking overhead.

He had to get to shore. His board was demolished. The next set was coming. The attacker would be waiting for him. And he was running out of air.

Taylor felt the world shift slightly. Just a gentle tug about his body, scarcely enough to pull at his position clutching the rock. But he knew what it signaled. His time was up.

He reached for his ankle and released the leash connecting

him to the remnants of his board. Using the rock as a base, he kicked off shoreward. The seabed came up fast here. He skirted another rock, then made for the surface.

He exploded into the shooter's view, gasping hard. Thankfully the shooter was searching over to his right, where the board bobbed in four pieces. Taylor grabbed two quick lungfuls and a single glimpse of the next incoming set. Then he dove, chased by another bullet.

The next wave tumbled him like he was caught in a gritty washing machine. Taylor smacked an underwater boulder so hard his arm went numb. But when the wave passed, he was able to twist about and find the bottom and stand. His head emerged through the froth. He was in neck-deep water. The next wave bore down with teeth of salt and foam. He could not afford a glance behind. The shooter would just have to wait his turn. He gulped air and ducked, gripping the nearest rock with his good arm.

The wave dislodged Taylor and shoved him shoreward. The next collision punched the air from his chest. When he came up again, he knew something wasn't right. Taking a breath stabbed him hard. He glanced shoreward and was cheered to see locals leaning over the cliffside edge and pointing down at the shooter's perch. A glance seaward was also reassuring, for riding the next wave in was Kenny, the Englishman. He was aiming straight for Taylor, but his gaze was on the shooter. As Taylor ducked under the incoming wave, he decided Kenny's arrival was both good and bad. Good, because it gave the shooter more to think about.

Bad, because Kenny seemed unsurprised by the shooter. Which meant he was on to Taylor and his mission.

Taylor tried to wedge himself between two smallish rocks. But the wave was too much for him in his present state. The wash dislodged him and tumbled him further inland. His head struck a stone. He felt a blinding pain and saw a sweeping wash of stars. The last sound Taylor heard was the music of bullets drilling into the water about him. His final thought was how sad it seemed to finally want to learn, only to have it all come too late.

Then he was struck yet again, and the entire world went away for good.

c h a p t e r 2

ELEVEN DAYS EARLIER, TAYLOR KNOX HAD ARRIVED at the Annapolis lab where he worked to discover that the rumors were indeed true. His nightmare was about to begin.

The front glass door sighed open to reveal the receptionist crying so hard she could not answer the phone. His coworkers walked aimlessly and spoke in muted tones, clearly awaiting news of their own demise. Taylor skipped the morning crush by the elevator and took the stairs. He had no interest in being doused in others' misery on a Monday morning.

Annapolis had two very distinct faces. The red-brick streets of the harbor region and historic old town were collectively known as Millionaire's Row. The city's western side was a different story. Western Annapolis was gradually spreading to merge with Crofton. And Crofton was dangerously close to northeast Washington. Northeast Washington was gang territory. Northeast Washington was why the capital had the nation's highest murder rate. Taylor's company, a medium-sized producer of specialty eye medicines, was located in an industrial park in Annapolis's western borderlands.

Taylor stood by his office window, looking out beyond the new high-tech buildings to where the sprawl began. He could walk out the front door, go five blocks west, and buy a fully automatic Uzi with explosive bullets. He found the prospect tempting. Five minutes past nine and the day was already that bad.

There was a knock on his open door. The division's lone secretary asked, "Did you hear?"

"I heard."

"You don't look surprised."

"Why should I be?" Taylor remained focused on the smoggy sunlight beyond his window. "The buzz has been going around for weeks."

"They've called a confab downstairs in the auditorium. Five minutes."

"You go ahead."

"This was more in the way of a direct command."

Each lab team was assigned one secretary. On paper, Allison Wright was supposed to work for everybody. But the division's lab techies had no idea how to deal with someone as stunningly beautiful as Allison. Her first two weeks in the office, they hounded her every movement. Allison responded with a laser glare and an arctic tone. Allison Wright clearly had a problem with male tribal habits. But she was also an excellent secretary, one Taylor had no interest in losing. So Taylor had intervened, letting it be known that techies were easier to replace than this particular secretary. He had eventually overcome Allison's distrust by ignoring it. She was a single mom raising a gorgeous four-year-old and trying hard to forget a man who had never been satisfied with what he had at home. The techies didn't know any of this because Allison didn't want sympathy. She wanted a chance. Taylor made no objections when the child needed her. He arranged training funds so Allison could attend university night classes. In return, Allison ignored the way the techies tracked her every move, flooded her e-mail with illicit suggestions, and referred to her as the division's ice goddess.

The chief scientist of Taylor's team met him in the hallway. "You heard?"

"Too much."

"You know them?"

"Not the company. The family."

"Is the lady as bad as they say?"

Taylor only accelerated. The scientist called after him, "Should I be dusting off my résumé?"

Inside the auditorium, he chose to isolate himself among strangers. But the talk among them was the same as he had been hearing from his own team.

The lights died and the chatter with it. Gerald Gowers, the company chairman, entered the spot over the podium. "I guess there's no need to tell you yesterday's news. You folks are just too sharp for me. Which I suppose is why we're such an outstanding team."

Taylor had met the CEO a few times. Most of the techies spoke of Gowers with respect. He was a nice enough guy for somebody holding the corporate ax. "A team," the chairman repeated. "That's what we are and what we will remain. The Revell Corporation is not acquiring us to cut out our heart. Revell wants us because we are the best at what we do. And we're the best for one reason only. That reason is you. So don't treat this as a threat, either to your positions or your projects. Revell needs you. Revell *wants* you.

"You know the situation we're facing. We're minnows swimming with the sharks. For us to survive in today's pharmaceutical market, we need size we don't have. We need to ally ourselves with a giant. My team has spent over a year searching for the perfect fit. We are convinced this partner should be Revell." He turned and nodded at a woman seated behind him. "Let me introduce Harriet Waters, senior vice president of Revell. I ask that you pay careful attention to what she has to say."

Gowers was replaced at the podium by a middle-aged woman with a perky bounce to her every movement. Even before she opened her mouth, Taylor knew that sending her as the company rep had been a bad mistake. She might work as a conduit to the executives. But techies were a peculiar breed. They could smell corporate doublespeak a mile away.

"We within the Revell family are just so happy to welcome you on board." She paused for a huge smile. Harriet Waters wore a shiny lavender suit, a white shirt, and an oversized crimson bow tie. She looked like a leftover Christmas package. "We like to think of ourselves as a great big happy clan, everyone pulling together to further the company aim. Which is to supply the best possible product each time, every time."

The entire row in front of Taylor sank lower in their seats. Harriet Waters began a glitzy show and tell projected on the big screen at the back of the stage, complete with a soundtrack of happy-sappy music and video tours of all nine Revell factories. The smallest Revell lab was twice the size of Taylor's entire company. Which of course left everyone swallowing hard over the realization of just how easy it would be for Revell to absorb, digest, and expel.

Taylor was approaching thirty years old, far too young to be stamped as expendable. He was the only guy on his team who was not a scientist. Taylor's title was project manager, a fancy name for a bean counter. His job was to keep tabs on the company's dime. His team liked Taylor because he was square with them, and because he watched their backs with the execs on the top floors.

The video presentation shifted to a head shot of Revell's chairman, Amanda Revell, daughter of the company's founder. Taylor could not hide his wince. The woman gave the camera as close to a smile as she could muster and said, "My name is Amanda Revell. Let me take this opportunity to welcome you to our company. Revell has a long and proud history of leading the way in numerous fields of pharmaceutical research. We currently sell a number of best-selling products, including the two most prescribed drugs in the world."

The smile slowly slipped away, as though the effort of holding it in place was too much. Or perhaps it was simply that she did not care enough to try. "I am confident that your group will help us bring to market the newest and the best. And you will do so on time and on budget."

The auditorium gave a collective shudder as the screen went blank. They knew the score. The scientists had been trading e-mails with their counterparts at Revell's labs. Revell's lab rats and techies all loathed Amanda Revell. She was a spiteful, rapacious executive with a reputation for cutting off projects that did not perform on time. She dressed in mannish dark suits and talked with a low burr. Revell's lab staff called her the Drag King.

Harriet Waters returned to the podium with a cheerleader's excited little hop. "Isn't she the greatest?" She paused, as though waiting for the gathering to rise and give a Japanese-style company cheer. "Well, I for one am thrilled to be working for such a dynamic executive. Because of her, Revell remains a cutting-edge corporate leader that goes from strength to strength in a highly competitive field. And I am certain that once you are a member of the Revell team, you will feel exactly the same."

Taylor doubted that sincerely. He for one would not be given the time. As soon as Amanda Revell was in charge, Taylor's career was toast. Amanda had loathed him for years.

THE SECRETARY'S STATION WAS SUPPOSED TO BE AT THE base of the glass wall separating the administrative section from the lab. But work had tended to suffer whenever Allison was visible. So the chief scientist had semivolunteered to take the public desk and give Allison the office next to Taylor's. Taylor had merely pointed out that the alternatives, either missing project due dates or losing Allison, were equally unthinkable.

As Taylor was leaving for lunch, Allison hung up her phone and waved him over. "You're wanted in the sponsor's box."

The sponsor's box was what the techies called the top-floor executive suites. "Did they say why?"

"They don't tell the help anything. You should know that by now. You want me to call around?"

"I guess not."

"What's the matter?"

"Nothing." He just hadn't expected his dismissal to come this fast.

Allison tended to wear office outfits as severe as her expression. Today's suit was a midnight blue of modest cut. A creamy silk blouse flickered into view as she shifted behind her desk. She often hid such feminine traces beneath dark armor. Taylor was the only office male on whom Allison did not turn the chilling edge of her voice and gaze. Taylor had no intention of ever trying to make time with Allison, which of course was why she trusted him even a little. Taylor already knew too much about beautiful women forced to barricade themselves against further wounds.

Allison said, "If the bad stuff is about to start, I'd rather hear about it from you than some top-floor hangman with his silk noose."

"I'm not being called upstairs because of you or the team." Taylor pulled his jacket off the hanger and slipped it on. "They're gunning for me."

"That's insane." When Taylor did not respond, she added, "You run the highest performing team in the company."

"Doesn't change a thing. Wish me luck."

Allison waited until he was at the door to reply. "I'll go one better. Come by tonight and I'll fix you dinner."

"Excuse me?"

"You strike me as a serious meat eater." Her normally steady gaze flittered about the room like a captured bird. "I cook a very mean steak."

Allison was a year or so older than him, and lovely as a rose in the final flush of full bloom. But now that her features had thawed, her eyes held a world of experience, the kind that left her wounded even when she tried to smile.

Taylor replied, "I don't think that's such a good idea."

She lowered her voice. "We're not talking commitment here, Taylor. I left those expectations behind a long time ago."

Today her chestnut hair was worn loose and spilling over one shoulder. The strands beckoned him to brush them away from her ivory neck. But the absence of hope in both her eyes and her voice stabbed deep. "Which is why I shouldn't stop by."

"Is that a definite?"

"I'm afraid so. But thanks."

"Not even for a drink?"

"I'm just flesh and blood, Allison. We both know it wouldn't end there."

Her expression held the sadness of a billion lies and lonely nights, and all the mistakes other guys like him had already made. "You always were too good to be true."

Taylor rolled off the door and headed out. Shame he couldn't live up to what she thought of him. But there was no reason to burst another lady's bubble by saying so.

TAYLOR USED THE ELEVATOR'S MIRRORED WALLS TO TAKE stock. He had been described as handsome and charming and magnetic often enough to accept them as true. His features were Mediterranean in a darkly balanced manner. He stared back at eyes lit by a slight and unfocused fire and asked the inevitable question. Why had he refused Allison's invitation? The answer was as poorly hidden as his scars. He had been down that road too often. The next morning's dust was already gathered in his mouth.

To Taylor's surprise, the secretary ushered him straight into the chairman's private office. The goodwill Gowers had shown from the podium was gone. Instead he was tight, nervous, and suspicious. "You Taylor Knox?"

"Yes sir."

"Thought I recognized you." He pointed Taylor to a chair. "You've got thirty seconds to tell me exactly what your connection is to the merger."

"None."

"Don't give me that." Gowers's out-of-season tan was stretched white around his eyes and mouth. "I should've known Revell would plant spies in my staff."

"Sir, that's not how things are."

"You have to do better than that."

Gowers's secretary knocked and announced, "They're ready for you."

"Right." Gowers bolted to his feet, waving Taylor to follow. "Let's go."

Taylor ignored the pair of mid-level corporate types who

swung in behind them. "The first definite word I had about the merger was this morning's announcement."

The chairman took the stairs and headed up. "So you won't even do me the courtesy of an honest answer."

"This has nothing to do with corporate espionage, Mr. Gowers."

"Save it." He slammed open the rooftop steel door so hard it hammered the concrete wall. He had to raise his voice to be heard over the helicopter's spinning rotors. "I've checked on you. Your team claims you're hot stuff. Now I know why. They think your insider position with Revell is going to save their hides!"

Taylor waited until the chopper had lifted off to shout, "Sir, it's not what you think."

The chairman turned to the window and shut him out. The chopper banked away from the city, passed over the inlet and a forest and a manicured golf course, and headed for the open sea. The Revell corporate logo on the six leather seats was all the explanation Taylor needed of what lay ahead.

Taylor Knox was a product of his past and scorned any man who claimed to have risen free of such ashes. He had a high respect for money, particularly since he had never had enough. Taylor was not a brawler by nature, but he had no fear of battle. He was tall and dark in the Minorcan manner and hard as the live oaks that surrounded his homeland. Once, when the rage was on him, Kirra Revell had told him all he needed was an eye patch and a cutlass to join the ranks of his pirate forebears.

His eyes were the only part of him that did not hold to the ancient Spanish heritage, a sky blue gift from his Irish daddy. But his father had been unable to overcome his own inheritance of a truly bad heart and had died when his son was just nine. Taylor had been left to fend for himself along the hardscrabble streets of North Town, the poor white trash region of St. Augustine, Florida. Taylor had been raised by any number of idle hands. They had taught him the Minorcan heritage of indentured slavery, as though hiring themselves out to Spanish overlords three hundred years earlier justified a life of drunkenness and drugs and gambling. He learned to handle a knife and his fists, how to gig for gators, and where to sell both the smoked meat and the skins. He netted fish and set lures and hunted out of season and raised bird dogs. At the ripe old age of eleven, Taylor had guided his first party out for largemouth bass.

But he was too smart to hide the pleasure he found in books, and too tough to be scorned for acing his schoolwork. He went to college on a scholarship. There was enough of the buccaneer in him to relish the convoluted patterns of modern accounting. He covered his living expenses with a variety of semilegal jobs until he landed the prized summer slot at the richest marina in northeast Florida. Which led him to Kirra Revell and dreams far beyond anything a poor Minorcan boy should ever have tried to claim.

As the chopper began its descent, the chairman leveled his gaze once more on Taylor. "The least you owe me is half a dose of the truth!"

"Sir, they told you to bring me along today because they want to make my firing as personal as possible."

"You worked for them?"

"In a manner of speaking."

"I checked your file this morning. There wasn't a word in there about a prior connection to Revell."

"That's because there wasn't any. Not to the firm." Taylor pointed out the chopper's window at a gleaming white yacht with smoked glass for eyes. "I worked on their boat."

The *Rapacious* was 250 feet long. Amanda was playing half-court basketball on the aft deck. The chopper set them down on the foredeck helipad and took off, all the while keeping well away from Amanda's game. She was too intent to even look over. But the well-dressed crowd on the middle deck all watched and pointed. In the distance, six sailing vessels competed for two available slots in the America's Cup trials. Amanda's sponsored boat was behind. Which was why Amanda was playing basketball and not watching the race. Amanda Revell never lost. If she was losing, she left the game.

Taylor loathed the Revell family yacht. Between his sophomore and junior years at university, he'd gotten the job as dock boy at the club marina where the *Rapacious* was moored. The following summer he'd been hired as galley goon. He had stayed on board through three summers, as the money was good enough to pay his keep at grad school. Then Amanda had caught him visiting her younger sister Kirra's forward cabin. The Revell family had not taken the news well that Kirra had fallen for a hired hand. Not well at all.

Oh yes, he knew this boat.

Taylor's blue blazer and club tie looked distinctly weary alongside the shipboard designer fashion. The other guests assumed he was a lackey brought to hold the CEO's files. Their gazes slipped off him like grease off a hot Teflon pan. Taylor had three summers' experience of being ignored. But it still rankled. Which was why he veered away from the chairman when they hit the middle deck. He snagged a glass from a passing waiter and worked his way through the memories. The middle deck was split between the open veranda where he stood and the shaded vestibule where the more delicate guests avoided the brilliant August sun. A thirty-foot bar ran across the back wall, tended by three hustling deck hands in white jackets and leathery tans. One of the bartenders spotted Taylor and flashed him a swift grin. Behind the bar opened the control deck, which even at anchor was staffed by crewmen in starched whites.

Then Taylor spotted Kirra's father wheeling over his chair. Taylor set his glass down on the railing. Such enemies needed to be met with both hands free.

"Why, you paltry little scum." Old man Revell spoke with

conversational ease, as though Taylor's presence was not even worth a decent rage. "What on earth are you doing here?"

"I'm guessing you're going to tell me that yourself, Jack."

"You will address your betters with proper respect."

"Happy to. Only I don't see any of them around."

The founder of Revell Pharmaceuticals rolled his chair a fraction closer. "When I heard you worked for this newest company Amanda went after, I was delighted. Do you hear me? Dee-lighted. I can't tell you how happy I am to have this opportunity to destroy you."

Taylor had long fantasized over what he'd like to say to the old man who had done so much to wreck his life. Only now they were surrounded by a hundred or so sparkling guests, and all eyes were on him. "Why, because your little girl showed good taste for once?"

The old man flushed scarlet. "Raymond!"

The largest of the deck hands slipped out from behind the bar and approached. "Sir?"

"Be so good as to toss this vermin to the sharks."

Raymond's smile had always been his easiest way of lying. "You going to come quietly?"

"Absolutely not."

"Be a good boy." Raymond had the moves of a blond puma. "Don't make a scene and we might even give you a ride to shore."

"Ah, but our dear Taylor revels in making scenes." The voice was instantly recognizable. But not the hand on his arm. To Taylor's recollection, Amanda Revell had never touched him before. "Daddy, call off your hound."

"You invited this parasite onto my boat?"

"Yes, and you know precisely why. Raymond, go back to the bar. Now."

The deck hand did not move until Jack Revell flicked his hand. Raymond straightened from his fractional crouch. "Always a pleasure, Taylor."

"Some other time."

Jack Revell's gaze was glacial gray and half submerged beneath scruffy eyebrows. "I'll never forgive you for what you did. Never."

Amanda tugged on his arm. "Come on, Taylor."

But her father was not finished. "You and your backwoods wiles twisted my little girl away from her family."

"Sorry, Jack. You'll have to dump that one on the man in the mirror."

"Taylor, leave it."

Taylor shook off Amanda's hand. "Kirra never was a part of the family power structure. She was too smart for that. She knew you for exactly who and what you are."

"All right, enough!" Amanda inserted herself between the two men. Her lithe spandex form was still perspiring from the game. "Downstairs!"

Taylor allowed himself to be turned and prodded toward the stairs. Anything was better than giving voice to what would have come next. Which was that Kirra's turning away from the family had been one of the many reasons why he had loved her so.

And still did.

From behind him, Amanda commented, "Shame on you, Taylor. Baiting the old man like that. I would have expected better."

"What can I say?" He halted when they entered the main lounge, a place of burl and Chinese silk and original oils. "The real target wasn't in range."

To his surprise, Amanda smiled. As though she were genuinely pleased with his response. She led him down the port hall to the office, held the door for him, then shut and locked it. "Have a seat, Taylor."

He remained standing. "Last time I was in this place was when your father gave me the ax."

"Sit. Please."

He stayed where he was. The room was the same as when her old man had commanded the desk. Taylor's roving gaze was halted by a blow-up of a photo that Kirra had carried in her wallet. Two blond girls swam in sparkling Caribbean waters, supported by a woman who could only be their mother. Kirra's mother had been an Australian dancer whom Jack Revell had spotted from his box in the New York City Opera House. Theirs had been a fairy-tale romance, all but the ending. She had died when Kirra had been just five. Leukemia.

The family had been devastated. Kirra had retreated into a world of her own making. Amanda had fashioned herself after her one remaining parent. Or so Kirra had said, on the few occasions she tried to explain how her older sister had turned out.

Amanda opened the fridge behind the desk and drew out an Evian. "Can I offer you something?"

"What is it you want, Amanda?"

"Same old Taylor." She was a fraction taller than Kirra and a good deal harder. Her eyes, her stance, her voice. Very similar to her younger sister, yet totally different. Kirra had been wrong to defend her sister. The reason Amanda had followed in her father's rapacious footsteps was because Amanda was Amanda. Always had been. Taylor had long since decided that when it came time to fit Amanda Revell for her final resting place, the embalmers would discover she had always had formaldehyde for blood.

But now, as he watched her unscrew the cap and take a long pull, Taylor found none of the expected rage. All he felt was the ashes of old shame over what he himself had done.

Amanda replaced the cap and rolled the bottle across her forehead. "Kirra's gone missing, Taylor."

"No surprise there." Prior to their becoming an item, Kirra had run away a lot.

Taylor had tried his best to talk Kirra into running away with him. But their relationship had also been marked by another major change in Kirra's life. One that had ended a great many of her wild ways. Kirra had started going to church. The family had been so dumbfounded by her transformation that they had not mocked her seriousness. Initially, Taylor had poured scorn over what he called her religious kick. That was before he realized it was the beginning of their end.

"This time it's different."

Taylor struggled to refocus. "So send in your corporate dogs."

"We did. They couldn't deliver."

"That's impossible."

"That's the way it is, Taylor."

"You're telling me she's been kidnapped?"

"We don't think so. There's been no ransom demand, nothing."

"Contact the authorities."

"We've done that too. Zilch. According to them, Kirra's an adult. If she chooses to leave, that's her legal right."

Taylor studied her. "What aren't you telling me?"

"The week after we brought in the FBI, Kirra sent a note. She was fine. That's basically all she said. She was fine and wanted to be left alone."

"So do what she says, for once."

"I don't think the letter was hers, Taylor. I know my sister better than anybody."

"You're wrong there."

Amanda shot him a hard look. Which did not bother Taylor at all. Amanda had never pretended any affection. Up front and straight ahead had always defined Amanda Revell. "I'm telling you the letter wasn't hers."

"You brought me here to find Kirra?" This was too rich. After the family had done everything they could to split them apart. "And old Jack is going along with this?"

"He doesn't have any choice. Neither do I." She offered him a bulky file. "Here's the deal. Do this or die a swift corporate death. Find her and win a stake in the merger."

"This is a bad idea, Amanda."

"I'll assign you a director's share. At current market valuation, you'll clear just over three million dollars."

"Getting mixed up with your family again would only cause us all a lot of pain."

She responded with a grimace. Then she shoved the file into his hands. "Just have a look."

Taylor turned for the door, wishing he was strong enough to toss the folder in her face and yell that he was gone. Finished. Saved from falling yet again.

But Amanda halted him with a grip on his wrist. She motioned to the lamp, the ceiling vent, the phone. She then made a crawling sign for bugs.

Amanda pointed at the folder's cover. On it was written a telephone number and a time, midnight to four in the morning. Below that was a final warning: *Tell no one.*

Taylor studied her eyes, so similar to Kirra's, and so utterly different. "Tell me this isn't a joke."

"I knew I could count on you." She picked a piece of paper from the desk, folded it twice, and slipped it into his jacket pocket. "I believe your ride is back."

Taylor left, worried despite himself by what he had seen in Amanda's gaze. Amanda was never frightened. Never.

When the chopper was in the air and headed back for land and the corporate tangle, Taylor drew out the note. He read the four words, then opened the file and pretended to read the contents. But in truth his fingers leafed through pages his mind could not take in. Amanda's note rang through his head the entire way home.

She asked for you.

chapter 3

THE NEXT MORNING, TAYLOR WENT TO THE OFFICE
only because he had no other logical destination. But the truth
was, his air-conditioned corner of the lab was as close to a real
home as he had. He did his best to lose himself in the press of
work, but without success. Even with his door closed, he heard
the whispers. Even when there was no sound but the sigh of
manufactured air, he could hear the talk swirling on all sides.
He did not shut the blinds over the interior glass wall because
he had no desire to be further separated from his corporate

world. So every passing eye cut his way, lingering only long enough to tell him they knew. Word had circulated about his journey on the chopper to the Revell boat. Since he was still around, it could only mean he had power they did not understand. This accusation isolated him far more than any closed door ever could.

Midmorning, Allison finally braved the portal. She delivered her excuse in the form of files he did not need to see and an acquisition request he would normally have signed at day's end. Taylor scrawled his signature and said, "You can tell them everything is normal. I thought I was being taken out there to be fired. Instead, they asked me to help out with something. It's not tied to the merger, and as far as I know, everybody's jobs are intact."

"It would sound better coming from you."

"I'll make the rounds at lunch."

But she did not retreat. "Are there any arrangements you want me to make?"

"Like what?"

"I don't know. Travel, contacts, anything? I'm basically sitting there twiddling my thumbs."

Taylor set down his pen. "What's going on, Allison?"

"Nothing except talk about the merger." Her tone was as neutral as her dove gray suit. "Time is hanging heavy, that's all."

One of Taylor's boyhood hunting partners had been a morose guide with one chalky eye and cheeks that always seemed two days away from his last shave. The man almost never spoke. Instead he taught the boy with tiny motions of one finger or his chin. Look there, the movement would say. Study and listen and learn. His regular clients often bragged about the guide's ability to read sign even before the animal laid it down. Taylor had often dreamed of gaining the same ability through osmosis and sheer stubbornness. Now, as he sat and watched Allison avoid his gaze, he knew.

"I might need some help later. I'll let you know."

He followed her from the office, touched her elbow, and pointed them out the lab's entrance and into the corridor. He did not speak again until they were down by the stairwell. "Tell me who's gotten to you, Allison."

The words were strained by the tension in her throat. "I hate this. I *hate* it."

He spoke in a hunter's voice, low and controlled. "Take your time."

"I need this job, Taylor."

"I understand."

"But you've always been good to me. Too good, if you want to know the absolute truth. It'd be easy to . . . Never mind."

"Somebody came by for a chat," he suggested, trying to make it easy for her. "They want to track my movements. They said you'd be taken care of if you just let them know where I go and what I do." He took her silence for assent. "Was it one of the goons from the sponsor's box?"

"No." She spoke to the outside window. "A man I've never seen before."

"Describe him."

"Definitely not your standard issue corporate clone. Almost as tall as you and really heavy. But not flabby. He moved too fast for a fat guy. One minute I was alone, the next he was standing there in front of my desk." She sounded glad to have it out. "Dark suit, dark shirt, dark tie. Hair cut so short I couldn't even see the color, maybe grayish-blond. To tell the truth I was so shocked I didn't really notice."

"And he told you to pass on information."

"He said he was working for Revell. He needed regular updates on your movements. He had a Revell company card."

"His name?"

"Ted Turner."

He almost laughed. "How original."

"Just the name and a telephone number. Do you want it?"

"No." Allison was probably the only one with the number, which meant if anyone else called she'd be dust and ashes. "Thanks, Allison. This helps me. A lot."

She shot him an apologetic look. "He gave me an envelope."

"Cash?"

"Two thousand dollars. That may sound like nothing to you."

"No, Allison. It doesn't."

"What do you want me to do?"

It was his turn to examine the rear parking lot. Despite a night spent tossing and telling himself he could walk away from this, his choices were limited to one. He was involved; he was going. Finished. "Book me on the first flight tomorrow to Jacksonville."

"No, I mean about the guy. And the money."

"The money's yours, Allison. And I want you to tell the guy everything." He wished he could erase the guilt in those lovely sad eyes. "I owe you."

"I feel so ashamed."

"Don't. You're a good person caught in an impossible net. Do what they ask and tell me what you can." He turned away from the window and toward the unattainable quest. Kirra. Thinking her name to the corporate shadows was enough to double his heart rate. "I'll protect you as best I can."

TAYLOR TOOK THE HIGHWAY OUT OF JACKSONVILLE'S AIR-port because it was the natural thing to do. Soon as he was free of the city's rush, however, he took an exit west and aimed for the calmer traces of U.S. 1. He had a hunter's love of quiet reaches. Besides which, he needed to spot his spotters. The last fifteen miles before St. Augustine, the road was empty enough for him to observe how one other car slowed with him.

He arrived at the stoplight where the town's outer perimeter sprawled like a loathsome bloom of garishly painted concrete and neon. Taylor busied himself with a street map. The car trailing him had no choice but to pull ahead, since they were blocking the other lane and could not hide in stillness. Taylor pretended not to notice them. Horns from his own lane finally jerked him into motion. Taylor roared past the watchers. These two passes and a quick inspection in his rearview mirror were enough. He had his quarry made.

The bridge over the San Sebastian River evoked too many emotions for Taylor to sort out just then. For years the narrow span had been the furthermost border of his invisible prison. Even when he left, it was on a temporary pass. He had been trapped by his heritage and his lack of material resources. He had returned simply because St. Augustine was as good a place as any from which to break free.

He did not want to return home, not while trailing a bevy of danger. On a whim he took the road leading straight into the old town and turned into the Hotel Casa Monica, a place he had visited only once before. He nodded to the young man who jumped to open his door, but his mind remained caught by the past.

One night Kirra's family had dined there. Taylor had hung around with his buddies in their starched bellhop uniforms and watched their eyebrows climb skyward when Kirra had appeared. That night Kirra had worn a dress made from pink and yellow clouds. It had swirled about her young body in beckoning folds. He had introduced her to his pals both to invoke their envy and because he wanted to remind Kirra just whom she was holding hands with, a boy born to life's back entrance. Kirra had only snuggled in closer, holding his arm with both hands, pressing her entire form to his as she laughed at something the bellhop had said. Then she had gently tugged him across the street to the town's central square. Beneath a tribute to the Revolutionary War prisoners the British had encamped on the same stretch of open ground, she had kissed him for the very first time. He could still recall the feel of her lips, and the smell of her perfume, and her taste of strawberries and youth.

This time, he took a suite because he could. The folder Amanda had given him had held an envelope containing five thousand dollars. There was also a super-thin cell phone, along with a driver's license and credit card made to Robert Pleasance. But when he placed the call, it was on the hotel phone and straight through the Revell switchboard.

There was a fractional hesitation when he gave Amanda's secretary his name. A series of patches told him Amanda was elsewhere than the corporate penthouse office. But she was on the line in a matter of seconds. Amanda answered as sharp as he had expected. "I told you after midnight!"

"Won't help. I've been made."

"What?"

"Isn't that the correct term? Excuse me. I'm new to the game of corporate espionage."

"You're being followed?"

"Two men. One of them looks like a shaved gorilla. The

other is a graybeard with wraparound shades. They're driving a silver Caddy. They've been on me since the J-ville airport."

There was a moment of muffled conversation, a pause, then she asked, "Where are you?"

"Casa Monica."

"What?"

"Sweet, isn't it? Thought maybe I'd send your old man a postcard."

Of all the reactions she might have given, the one he least expected was to hear her rusty laugh. "Pop was right. You're too nasty to hang."

"These must be your hired hands. I recognize the sullen expression that comes from working for your family."

"If they are, I'll have their hides for wallcoverings. Give me their license plate."

He did so. "You want me to believe you're not behind this?"

"My security people resent you being called in. They claim they can handle this better on their own."

"Maybe they can."

"They've had their chance. Stay right where you are." She clicked and was gone.

Five minutes later she came back with, "They insist it's not them."

"So they say."

"I've ordered them to prove they're not involved by getting rid of your tail. In one hour or less."

"Amanda, who else would want to keep Kirra hidden?"

"Not now."

"Amanda—" But the line was dead.

TAYLOR REFUSED TO BE HURRIED, THOUGH THE TENSION in Amanda's voice remained with him like a cord knotted around his chest. He sat in the lobby, where he found comfort in the multitude of both people and exits. The hotel was Andalusian in architecture and old money in splendor. He was surrounded by the sort of people who could take such things for granted. As though they had been deeded a special ride through life, a ticket fashioned from Persian carpets, hand-painted tiles, indoor fountains, high-back Cordovan leather chairs, and gold-embossed ceiling beams. As though their entitlement was so great that they recognized no authority greater than the one they carried in their wallets.

He went through the file once more. The detectives used the desperate tone of a team one step from having their financial plug pulled. We're so close, all we need is another week, another ten thousand dollars, another five people. Somebody's job was definitely on the line here.

One item stood out even after Taylor shut the file. Kirra had gone back to school. She was attending Flagler College, taking courses in local history. She had also been working with a certain Father Pellecier on an undisclosed honors project. The professor had refused to disclose what she had been studying, other than to say she had been reviewing documents dating back to the first Spanish period. Taylor doubted that this had anything to do with her disappearance, but he found the information unsettling. It magnified the distance he felt from the only woman he had ever loved.

The phone rang. Amanda said, "They're gone."

"Don't ever hang up on me again."

Clearly she was not accustomed to being addressed in such a fashion. "Don't you even care about your stalkers?"

"I'd be more interested in knowing who they are and how your men got to them so fast."

"Call me tonight."

"Add to that an explanation of who is after your sister."

"If I knew that, I'd be halfway to where I didn't need to be talking with you." She bit off the words with increasing terseness. "Now if you'll excuse me, I have a two-billion-dollar company to run."

"I know why you called me in. Your detectives followed the standard path and got nowhere. I assume you told them as little as you're telling me." When she remained silent, he added, "You either give me some explanations, Amanda, or I'm walking away from this."

She breathed a moment, long enough that he worried she might call his bluff. Which it was. There was no way he could turn away until he knew Kirra was all right. Much as he might want otherwise.

But all she said was, "Midnight."

Taylor left the hotel and headed north on foot. Flagler College's ornate Spanish colonnades and towers powered above the surrounding palms. Taylor took George Street and threaded his way through sweltering tourists. His mind felt as heated as his body, compressed by flavors of a past he both loved and despised.

The woman he was going to see was a former neighbor, now relocated to an apartment block with a view of the Intracoastal Waterway. Ada Folley was both Minorcan and octoroon, the result of discrimination practiced against two equally reviled races. In the sixteenth century, Minorcans had been brought over by the original Spanish settlers to clear the land and drain the swamps and build their fortress. The Spaniards had offered them an impossible boon. Serve the king for seven years and they would earn both freedom and land. The Minorcans were a fiercely stubborn race of mercenary fighters. They had survived, gained their freedom, and put down roots in the rich black soil between the Matanzas and San Sebastian Rivers. After the Civil War they had been joined by freed slaves desperate for what the Minorcans had won two centuries before. Their Yankee administrators had deeded these newcomers bottom land at the growing city's southern end. St. Augustine thus stood in haughty blindness between the two settlements, the Minorcan's North Town at one end and Lincolnville at the other.

Ada Folley and her Minorcan shrimper of a husband had formerly lived two houses down from Taylor. She was a taciturn woman with a eye so cold it could halt the scorn of racist neighbors before it was ever uttered. When Taylor had been a child, he had heard rumors that Ada's mother had practiced *juju,* the old slave magic. But Ada was a religious woman, and the only time he had worked up the courage to ask her if it was true, she had slapped his face so hard his ears had rung all afternoon.

"Don't go giving speech to the shadows, you," was all she had said at the time.

As Taylor climbed the stairs to her apartment, he recalled the only other time Ada had struck him. It had been two days before his sixteenth birthday. He had just been accepted onto the high-school varsity football team, and that same afternoon a cheerleader had claimed him for her own.

Ada had drawn him from the street with, "Come over here, child. I want to see what it is you're growing into."

At six feet, Taylor stood five inches taller than Ada. He was also as cocky as any fifteen-year-old who had just been kissed by the prettiest girl at school. But Ada Folley carried herself with a severe dignity that brooked no dissent. Taylor did as he had been told.

"Stop right there." She leaned over the porch railing and squinted at where he stood in the front garden's brightest island, the only spot not shaded by the pair of blooming magnolias. "You coming up on a birthday, ain't that right?"

"Day after tomorrow."

"How old you coming up on, twelve?"

"I'll be sixteen and you know it."

"Bet you think you're too big to be running down to Ada's for her peach cobbler, you."

"I'll never get too old for that." Ada cooked for the Revell family and was known as the finest chef on three islands. When the wind was right, her baking slowed traffic out on Highway 1. "You got one ready now?"

"Stop your dancing and stand still, child." Light glinted off piercing dark eyes. "I got me the feeling you gonna start breaking some hearts. Yes, I can hear the weeping now. They's gonna be tears shed up and down the islands, on account of the sweet boy the ladies will *think* they see in you."

Something in those half-lidded eyes brought to mind the rumors of Ada's mama, the fortune-teller and Lincolnville witch who had planted curses in her backyard garden next to her runner beans. But Taylor was cocky enough to sweep his hair off his forehead and pretend he could not feel the fear rippling through his gut like wind over calm waters. "Well, all right."

She leaned back into the shade. "Set yourself down here beside me, boy."

"I got to be getting—"

"You ain't got nothing to do nowhere 'cept right here beside me."

Grudgingly Taylor eased himself down on the top stair. "So I'm here. Now what?"

"You got some lip on you; I give you that." The old rocker shifted beneath her. "You ever thought maybe you could save them ladies and yourself a whole heap of grief, give Jesus a chance to do His work?"

"Figure maybe I'll do myself some living first."

"That what you call sowing seeds of misery, living?"

He felt scalded by her scorn. "Sure sounds a lot better than what you got on offer. Crawling round on my knees don't look like all that much fun to me."

The slap came out of nowhere. A striking snake had nothing on Ada Folley. "You best be minding your manners. Ain't nobody gonna sit on my front porch and go disrespecting the Lord, no."

He felt like he'd been struck with an oak stave, her hand was that hard. "What'd you do that for!" Taylor had to shout the words to keep from weeping. "That hurt!"

"On account of it was meant to. Now you be listening good, boy. I stood and held your hand the day your daddy was laid to rest. I love you like you's one of my own. I know you had it hard, and I know you got every good reason to carry your load of burning coals. But it ain't worth it; you hear what I'm saying? I know what I'm talking about, me. I know all there is to know about harboring reasons to go revenging on this dark earth."

"I got to be going." Taylor stumbled across the yard. His back to the woman, he still refused to raise his arm and strike away the tears.

She chased him down the road with, "Mark my words, boy. You ain't gonna be burning nobody but your own sweet self."

ADA'S APARTMENT BUILDING STOOD ON THE SAME reclaimed wetland as the city's assisted living center and nursing home. The buildings were separated from Lincolnville's southernmost side by a broad swath of shallow lakes and marsh islands, now a dedicated bird sanctuary. Taylor climbed the open staircase and knocked on Ada's door. To his right, the westering sun burnished the marshes into a bas-relief of gold and heat.

The woman did not appear to have aged a day. Nor lost a trace of her snappish air. "Been wondering when you'd come skulking round here."

"Hello, Miss Ada."

"Your momma know you in town?"

"No ma'am."

"Then I guess I don't need to ask how you be doing." She turned and stumped into the kitchen. "You eaten today?"

"I'm fine."

"I ain't asked you that. I asked, have you eaten."

The smell of fresh baking took him back what seemed like

a thousand years. "I'd never turn down whatever you're offering. You know that."

She sliced him a piece of pie the color of old tar. "Get yourself into that while I make a fresh pot."

Nowadays the dish was referred to by the ten-dollar name of flourless chocolate cake. Taylor knew it by the less elegant title of mud pie. He seated himself on a stool by the counter and dug in. "This is incredible."

"Can't be a good thing, losing sight of your manners so you talk with your mouth full." She set a mug and a napkin down in front of him. "How you be taking your coffee?"

"Black is fine, thanks."

"Like your daddy." She stood watching him eat, then retrieved the dish and fork. "More?"

"No thanks, Miss Ada."

"Your daddy had himself the finest smile I ever saw on a man. Folks who didn't even like him loved him. Spent all his life one step away from goodness. Like his son." When the coffee gurgled, she poured him a mug. "Seeing a new lady, you?"

Taylor shook his head, no.

"Why is that, I wonder? You done grown into the fine-looking boy I knew you'd be."

He tasted his coffee. "I got tired of being alone whether I was with someone else or not."

There was probably some Indian blood somewhere in Ada's heritage. She had such high cheekbones her eyes were pressed up into almost Oriental slits. Which only accented the intensity of her gaze. "Sounds to me like you still be carrying Kirra's flame in your heart."

"Do you know where she is?"

"Gone. That's all I can say for certain. This time maybe gone for good." Without asking, Ada refilled his mug. "I love that girl like she was my own brood. Loved her and raised her and taught her to cook. Seeing that girl give her life to Jesus was the finest moment of my *life*."

Which, if truth be known, had been part of their problem. Especially after Kirra went and changed the rules. But Taylor knew better than to start down that road. Not with Ada Folley. "Her family's worried about how Kirra's gone missing."

"Like they shoulda been back when she was young enough for it to still matter."

"I've got no argument with that."

"Well, I still got me a quarrel with you." Her hands gripped a dishrag and began polishing a counter that already shone. "You tore that poor girl's heart to pieces."

"I could say the same thing about what she did to me, and you know it."

"Almost two years on and you still ain't faced the truth. You was the one went playing around with that Jezebel. Not Kirra."

"But Kirra *was* the one who broke up with me, Ada. You remember that little detail?"

"I remember how you two always seemed to be either going

apart or coming back together. I remember the sparks. I remember the *love*."

That much was true. Their relationship had constantly been marred by quarrels. Taylor had had every reason to play the angry young man. And Kirra had been wild enough in her own right, rich and willful and rebellious. At least, she had been until her conversion.

Kirra possessed a dancer's verve and temper, fiery and larger than life. Some of her strongest compliments had been delivered as wounding barbs. Taylor sipped coffee now flavored with bile and recalled their final argument. The apartment rang with what Kirra had shouted. *Faith has taught me to honor what is real, and you are the most real man I ever met.* To have her offer such praise in a rage had left Taylor leaking real blood.

Taylor realized Ada was watching him. He said, "We never broke up like that before."

She huffed her disagreement. "I know what I saw. You was like two angry magnets. Seemed like every time I turned around you'd be pulling apart. Then you'd fly back together in a whirlwind of love, just *sick* over all them hours you were apart."

"Six days," Taylor replied, still burning from old loss. "That was the longest we'd ever been apart before. This time was six *weeks*."

Agony. The time apart had been pure torture. Six weeks she had remained isolated behind her walls of wealth and anger.

Then the woman had appeared. Jezebel, Ada had called her. The name was as good as any. She had been everything Kirra was no longer. Wanton and voluptuous and available. Taylor had come in from a surf and found her sprawled on a towel, basted in oil, wearing the tiniest bikini he had ever seen. How those three triangles had managed to stay in place was a mystery that bore close inspection. She had offered him the same sort of scrutiny, her green eyes sparked with an eagerness that inflamed.

Taylor had not been with a woman since Kirra's conversion. Her refusal to accept their mutual desire any longer had been yet another constant battle zone. Taylor had a well-honed desire for sex. He was handsome, athletic, and used to getting what he wanted. At least, he had been until Kirra had started attending church with Ada. For eight months he had subsisted on Kirra's religious version of a bread-and-water diet.

Jezebel. That night he had feasted on the woman with a lust as strong as rage. At dawn he had fled the woman's hotel room as he would have his own pyre.

Three days later, a buddy who still worked on the Revell yacht told him of the shrieking and moaning everyone had heard coming from the owner's cabin. Rumors flew. About Taylor. About another woman. About treachery and ruin.

Then the lawyers had arrived, bearing letters signed by Kirra herself. Taylor had been ordered never to come around again, not to contact her, not to call. Ever.

Ada was not finished. "She couldn't believe it when they told her you'd been with that other woman. What was her name?"

"I don't remember."

She sniffed a whole world of disdain. "Like to break my heart, hearing Kirra cry like that. Seemed like days I held that baby girl. Just sobbed and sobbed, clutching them awful pictures, I had to pry her fingers loose."

Taylor stiffened. "What pictures are you talking about?"

"Your mind's caught by the wrong hook, you."

"Kirra had photographs? Of me and that woman?"

"It ain't what she was having or not having. It's what you been *doing*."

"I should have known." Dormant embers reignited in full force. Taylor had spent countless hours fretting over how Kirra had heard about him and the other woman. There was only one place she could have obtained pictures of that night. "Why didn't you tell me this before?"

"On account of how it's not important." What she saw in Taylor's gaze caused her to add, "On account of how you'd probably go out and follow one stupid act with another."

Fitting the pieces together after almost two years still blistered his mind. "Amanda had detectives photograph me. Then she gave the pictures to Kirra."

"Look at me, son. What does that matter?" She took aim with a rigid finger. "Fact is, you were the one caught lying there in Jezebel's arms. You're the one broke that child's heart. All on account of you never learning the first lesson of a good life. The *only* lesson."

"I'm going to find her, Ada."

"What if she don't want finding? What if she don't want finding by *you?*"

"I hear different."

"Is that so? Who from?"

"Amanda."

Ada laughed out loud. "You be taking her word?"

"Why would she lie about this?" His thoughts burned with crystal clarity. "You know as well as anybody what she and old Jack Revell think of me. But she came to me, Ada. Think what that must have cost her. *She* came to *me.*"

Ada pulled the pot off the burner and emptied it into the sink. "I don't trust that woman a single solitary inch, no."

"The family thinks Kirra might be in real trouble. I need to see if that's true. If she is, I want to help."

Ada mulled that over a time. "You know she's been studying over to the college."

"Flagler. Yes."

"There's one professor she was always going on about. A monk, goes by the name of Pellecier. A good man, is what I hear. Best go talk with the father, you." A glint of heated iron shone from her gaze. "Maybe he'll be showing you what you never saw fit to learn from me."

MIDWAY BACK TO TOWN, TAYLOR PLACED THE CALL TO Amanda. But when the phone started ringing, he shut it off.

This was something he wanted to handle in person. He entered downtown almost glad for the closeness and the heat. It suited his mood right down to the bone.

Flagler College was built in the same ornate Spanish style as the hotel. The college was a lovely place drawn from a well of deep pockets and lined with a heritage that had nothing to do with Taylor. He might call this his hometown, but there was little he held in common with this college or its haughty air.

The halls were mostly empty, as he had caught the place in the humid interlude between summer school and the fall term. He found a lone administrator enclosed within her air-conditioned tomb, resentful over her confinement and the day she was missing. "Yes?"

"I am looking for Father Pellecier."

"And you are?"

"Taylor Knox."

"I'm sorry, the name means nothing to me. Are you a former student?"

"No."

"A visiting official, perhaps?" Her eyes held the gleam of one who had spent hours waiting for the chance to put someone down. "A job seeker? Because we do not normally give out information to people who just wander in off the street."

"I am here on behalf of the Revell family and foundation."

From the woman's response, he could only assume that the

college was among the foundation's recipients. "Do you have some ID?"

He handed over a company card. She studied it, undoubtedly hoping for sign of forgery. "Father Pellecier is away for the summer."

Taylor opened the folder to the back page, which was a transcript of Kirra's last three terms. "Can you tell me if any of these other teachers might be in town?"

"Where did you get that?"

"From the family."

"Student's transcripts are confidential material. Are you another one of those detectives?"

"I am not."

"Because I'll tell you the same thing I told them. You can't come traipsing in here and expect me to give you a solitary thing."

"Could you describe the detectives to me, please?"

"Certainly not. If the family wants information about one of our students, they can go through proper channels." She raised her voice as he started for the door. "Don't you turn around when I'm talking to you!"

Taylor shut the door and spotted a janitor grinning at him from further along the hall. "How you doing?"

"Better than you, I 'spect," the janitor chuckled. "Miz Landy's a piece of work, ain't she?"

"I bet the students all adore her."

"Yeah, they gots some different names for her. But I ain't gonna be saying them, no."

"I can imagine." Taylor extracted the transcript. "Do you know if any of these people are around?"

The janitor wore a gray coverall that up close smelled of floor polish and summer sweat. "Sure. Dr. Preston, he's most always here. Near 'bout lives in his lab, that man."

"Where do I find him?"

"Environmental sciences. They gots themselves a new building down off Treasury Street. You know where that is?"

"Sure."

"Go round back. Dr. Preston, he don't answer the front door for nobody."

"You wouldn't know where Father Pellecier's gone for the summer?"

"Same place as every other holiday, I 'spect. He keeps track of all them old books over to the city historical society."

"The building down on the waterfront?"

"That's the one." He went back to his mopping. "Loves them old books, that man. Knows more about this town than any man alive."

Taylor left the college's main building by the north exit and headed straight for the river. The city's historical society was housed in one of the oldest surviving homes, built by a merchant voyager a century and a half before America became a nation. When he buzzed and explained who he was and why he was there, the receptionist refused to open the door. When he buzzed again, she offered to have the police escort him away.

Taylor stepped from the porch and paused beneath the shade of a live oak. Clearly Amanda's detectives had left a bad taste in more than one person's mouth. He was unoffended by the reactions only because he was so irate with Amanda herself. She might be able to repair the damage her minions had wreaked here in St. Augustine, but there was no hope of her ever mending fences with Taylor. None.

Taylor recrossed the street and headed back inland. Newcomers were charmed by the quiet brick streets and the old cedar houses and the Spanish moss and the rivers and the rich architecture. The older families watched as their neighborhoods became picked clean of lifelong friends. Taylor walked streets made ever more unfamiliar by imported money. Pickups in driveways were being replaced by Porsches. Wind chimes sang where once old rockers had creaked. And not a single voice greeted him along a street he had once claimed as his own.

The spector of Amanda Revell stalked the superheated afternoon right beside him. That she had ordered detectives to follow him came as no surprise. That she had shown photographs of him and another woman to her own sister left Taylor limping in pain and rage.

Taylor was so wrapped up in the newest addition to the Revell saga that he didn't see them until they attacked.

One minute the road was empty. The next, a dark van

pulled alongside him. The rear door slid open and three men jumped out.

Taylor fought the arms that tackled him. Then one of the others hit him with something, a pipe or a hammer or a stave.

He did not pass out completely. Not until they bundled him into the back of the van and struck him again.

chapter 4

TAYLOR AWOKE TO DARK AND PAIN AND A SEWER'S
stench. He did not rise. His head thundered so that even the
slightest motion nauseated him.

Even clawing his fingers through the slime caused star
bursts behind his eyes. Taylor drifted in and out of conscious-
ness. His clearest thought was that this made as fitting a place
as any for his tomb.

When he next awoke, he was far more alert. Which was not
altogether a good thing. Because with the keener awareness
came a greater sense of fear.

Taylor opened his eyes but saw nothing. Even in the pitch black, he knew exactly where he was. The smell alone was enough to take Taylor back to earlier times. He had played here for years. He knew it well enough to know that his fear was justified. The water sloshing below his slimy perch was all the warning he needed.

He was positioned on a stone ledge scarred by decades of carvings and lumps of old candle wax. The slime came from the sea that twice each day rose to cover his shelf.

Slowly he pushed himself up to a sitting position. Everything hurt, especially his head. He touched the back of his skull and felt a sticky warmth where the attackers had struck him. But he was far more troubled by the seawater that drenched his feet when he swung his legs over the ledge.

Taylor felt along the damp wall behind him. He extracted a loose brick that had been used as a hiding place by generations of local children. He pulled out the waterproof container of matches and the larger one of candles. He struck a match. Even before he got the candle going, he knew he was in very serious trouble.

The Minorcans' first task for their Spanish masters was to build the fort where Taylor now sat. The Castillo de San Marcos was a star-shaped masonry fortress, the oldest in America. It was positioned upon a *camino cubierto*, a man-made spit of land between the outer islands where St. Augustine Beach and Vilano Beach now stood. The fortress looked directly into the open waters between them, situated where it could protect the deepwater channel and the empire's maritime fleet.

The fortress dungeons had two ways in. The main door was nail-studded and ancient. Tourists were brought to the tight stone stairs, shown the door and the rusting chains, and told of the Spaniards' cruelty to their indentured Minorcan slaves. But there was a second way in, a tunnel whose secret was passed on from one generation of kids to the next. Three centuries back, seawater had entered the dungeons and cleared away the refuse with each tide. Nowadays, however, sinking foundations and rising tidal currents meant the chamber filled to the top. Taylor felt the water edge higher up his shins and knew the tide was coming in. Waves boomed against the outer opening, sloshing water through the chamber with the noise. It was only a matter of time.

Holding his candle high, he dropped off the ledge. The water was almost waist deep, the currents strong enough he needed his free hand to keep his balance. He waded across to the stairs leading up to the door. Of course it was locked. He turned and stared at the opposite wall. The tunnel through which tides surged was completely underwater. But he saw it anyway.

For kids of nine or ten, the tunnel was a tight run of maybe forty feet. The last time he had crawled through was at fourteen, lured by a girl who promised him enough to make him do the impossible. He had been a skinny kid, little more than bones and muscle and testosterone. Even so, he had scraped away skin coming and going.

Driven by desperation, he waded toward the opening. The closer he came, the stronger surged the currents. He found a handhold on the slimy wall. Bracing himself so as to keep the candle aloft and alight, he measured with one foot. The aperture was impossibly small. Hot candle wax encrusted his fingers as he made his way back to the ledge. He wrapped up the remaining matches and candles and fitted the brick back into place. If he didn't make it out, he'd want to face his demise with at least a trace of flickering light.

He took another look around his prison, then planted the candle on the ledge. He forced himself forward, working against a current that grew stronger with each thunderous wave. His breath was a heaving bellows fueled by fear.

He submerged and checked out the opening with his hands. The tunnel's confines made him gag. The next booming rush of water was strong enough to dislodge his hold and push him back ten feet. He came up into utter dark and realized the tide had surged over the ledge, extinguishing his candle.

The blackness was suffocating now. He breathed deep. Over and over. He pushed away the fear as best he could. When the current began sucking back, he went down, extending one arm above his head and clenching the other by his side. Even so, he had to jam himself in.

He clawed his way forward. There was just enough room

for him to crawl slightly with wrist and elbow and knee and ankle. He scrabbled inch by inch, jamming back with his feet, scraping with his toes, reaching forward with his one hand. He stared bug-eyed at nothing.

Midway through he became jammed so tight he could not move at all. Not an inch. The harder he struggled the tighter he was trapped. He could not move either forward or back. Taylor opened his mouth and screamed his frantic fury. He broke free because the expelled breath shrank him just enough.

Only now his lungs were heaving great reflexive lunges for air. His entire body burned with the need to breathe.

He became wedged tight a second time. Then his forward hand felt the sharp-edged stone border. The tunnel's end was just ahead. He ripped and twisted and finally caught a fraction of a ledge with his toes. He pried himself forward two more inches. He took a firmer grip on the ledge and hauled with all his might. One leg of his trousers ripped as he scrambled out.

His arms reached together toward the silver illumination overhead. He kicked and swam with his back arched like a bow, his mouth already opened to take the breath he had to have *now*.

He exploded into the air, flying up so hard he emerged almost to his waist. He shouted gulping gasps of breath. The fortress was a looming shadow cut from the stars.

Perhaps he saw a human silhouetted on the ramparts. He could not be sure. When his vision fully cleared, the image was gone. The old place was said to house an army of ghosts.

chapter 5

TAYLOR'S RIPPED TROUSERS AND SHIRT MADE THE
sound of wet laundry in the wind as he walked. But there was
no wind that night, nor did he see a living thing. This was by
choice. He headed north from the fort, making his way
through the cypress and wild palms that bordered Matanzas
Bay. Up ahead was sanctuary in the form of another North
Town escapee, a young woman with whom he had stepped out
briefly, back before Kirra had captured his heart. Taylor had to
repeatedly halt and support himself on whichever tree was

closest at the time. His vision came and went in waves. His thoughts swirled worse than his eyesight.

The woman's home was at the base of a curved cul-de-sac. Beyond the neatly trimmed lawn and the sparkling pool he could make out the lights of Vilano Beach glimmering in the distance. The night was a vast summer swath of heat and crickets and lightning beyond the horizon. A faint breeze brought in the strong odors of wetland muck as he rang the front bell.

He heard the rapid tripping of young footsteps and instinctively backed far into the shadows. A blond-headed cherub in cartoon pajamas with red feet opened the door. Taylor did not recognize his own voice as he said, "Is your momma home tonight?"

A man's voice called from further inside, "Who is it, honey?"

"A man, but he's standing out where I can't see him good."

That brought the father in a hurry. "Get back inside the house."

"He wanted mommy."

"I said get inside." He put himself between the child and harm's way. "Who's out there?"

At that point his strength simply vanished. Taylor caught himself on a knee and both hands. "It's Taylor, John."

"Taylor Knox?" The man approached in a cautious sideways manner. "What've they done to you, boy?"

The child cried from the doorway, "I'm scared, Daddy!"

"I told you to get inside the house!" He raised his voice even higher. "Ruth! *Ruth!*"

"What is it?"

John fitted one strong hand under Taylor's arm and lifted. "Come on, old son, help me now." Then he said to his wife, "Go flip the switch on the garage doors."

"Why don't you just—"

"Do what I say. And bring your doctor's bag. And get the child upstairs!"

The garage door ground up at their approach. Taylor said, "I'm getting blood all over your clothes."

"Don't worry about that, now."

Ruth was a solid woman with the no-nonsense air of an emergency room doctor. Even so she could not keep the shock or the question out of her voice. "Taylor?"

"You were the closest to hand and the only folks I thought I could reach."

The man swept a half-finished bookshelf and a mess of tools onto the floor. "Honey, pull a towel out of the hamper and spread it out."

His wife was already moving. "Who did this to you?"

"I don't know. All I saw was a mask and a stave."

John peeled off what was left of Taylor's shirt and winced at the lacerations on his chest. "How come you're all wet?"

"They dumped me in the bay. Sort of."

"John, go call the police."

"There's not a lot I can tell them," Taylor said.

John talked as he dialed. "Man I haven't seen in over a year comes stumbling out of the night looking like somebody's gone over his body with razor wire, you bet I'm getting the cops in here."

Ruth found the place on his skull. "Is your vision blurry?"

"To tell the truth, I couldn't say." Now that he was down and people were watching over him, his eyelids came into a will of their own. "What time is it?"

"Just gone nine."

"That's impossible." He felt like it should be near dawn, so much had happened.

John set down the phone. "Cops are on their way." He returned to stand over Taylor. "Folks always did say you'd come to a bad end."

"You hush up, they did not." Ruth worked her way down to his leg. Whatever she found there caused her to raise her voice. "What did they do to you?"

"You remember the old dungeon." They were locals. He did not need to frame it as a question.

That brought horror to both their faces. "They stuck you in there? How'd they get you past the guards at the front gates?"

"I didn't have a chance to ask them. I was out at the time."

Ruth dabbed his leg with something that felt like painted fire. "You're too big to make it through the tunnel."

"I know."

"Does this have something to do with that rich Revell woman you took up with?"

Taylor chose that moment to surrender. His eyelids fell, and he took his answer with him into a dark cocoon.

A DREAM ABOUT THE TUNNEL WOKE TAYLOR IN THE MIDDLE of the night. This time he clawed his way forward only to confront something that forced him *back*. What it was precisely, Taylor never saw. The tunnel was pitch black and filled with bottom silt. But something was there. It filled the confines totally, gripped him with impossible strength, and held him there. Forever.

Taylor awoke drenched with the terror he had not admitted to until now. He padded to the guest bathroom, washed his face, toweled off the fear sweat, and returned to bed. As he slipped back into exhausted slumber, he found himself recalling something Ada Folley had told him years before. It was one of the few times Ada had ever made reference to her juju forebears. She had done it only because Taylor had kept pestering her, wanting to know if there was any truth to the rumors.

You want to know about the dark, do you? That was how Ada had finally responded, her eyes burning with a fire black as his recently departed nightmare. You want to touch that forbidden fruit? You best be watching out for the soon-to-come, is all I can tell you. The soon-to-come's right out there, hiding in shadows so thick you'll never see him till he pounces. But he's there all right. If you're sick, or somebody you love is coming close to that final door.

Taylor heard Ada's chant echo through his softly pounding head. Her voice sang him away to a dark that was something more than sleep. Cold as winter moonlight, the soon-to-come's breath. You best be ready, 'cause the soon-to-come is gonna call on you. Calls on everybody, and always when they ain't quite disposed to go. Oh yes. Be ready.

WHEN TAYLOR NEXT OPENED HIS EYES, HE WAS GREETED by birdsong and the sweet scent of bed linen dried in the open air. He inspected his wounds in the guest bath, felt the threads dangling from his head and left thigh, tested his joints, and knew he was going to be all right.

He showered and joined the family for breakfast, accepted their questions, and made no objection as John called the police back in. He forced himself to eat slowly, though he was as ravenous as a wolf and felt almost as scruffy. John was a big man and his borrowed sweats fitted Taylor like they were meant for two of him. At the table's opposite end, their daughter sang of sunrises and daffodils and entertained them with butterfly shadows her father helped her shape. Taylor observed the family's morning routine and felt worse than an intruder.

The policeman arrived just as they were finishing breakfast.

He was vaguely familiar, a man Taylor had last seen beneath the helmet of an opposing team. He had skin so black it was almost purple, and was big in the manner of someone who worked hard to keep his weight under control. Taylor told the entire story both because he owed it to his hosts and because there was nothing to be gained by holding back.

The cop made careful notes and kept his voice level for the child playing in the next room. "You got anybody can confirm what you been up to?"

"You mean, other than Amanda Revell?"

"I'll be in touch with them. But I was hoping for somebody closer to home, if you know what I mean."

"I'd just gone to see Ada Folley."

His face brightened. "Where you know Ada from?"

"She cooks for the Revell family."

"Sure, I knew that. How's that lady doing?"

"Nasty as ever."

"I hear you." He slapped his notebook closed and rose to his feet. Instantly the room shrank two sizes. "Where can I reach you, I need something more?"

"I've got a room at the Casa Monica."

John whistled. "You been moving up in the world."

"It's on the Revell nickel."

"John, good to see you again." The cop offered Taylor a hand and a hard eye. "Where have I seen you before?"

"I played tight end for Augustine High."

"Now I remember. You were the kid with all the moves."

"You gave me a couple of good licks our last game."

"Didn't stop you from making that winning touchdown." He nodded a farewell to the doctor. "Thanks for the coffee, Ruth."

He paused at the door and asked Taylor, "You think maybe the Revell daughter's been abducted?"

"All I can say for certain is somebody doesn't want her found. In the worst way."

The cop mulled that one over, then said, "Glad to see you ain't lost your moves."

When the cop had departed, John announced, "I'm late for the office."

Taylor heard the unspoken question. "If it's okay, I'd like to make a phone call. Then I'll be on my way."

Ruth responded in the formal manner of one guided by generations of southern protocol. "You're welcome to stay on here, Taylor."

"I'm fine, Ruth. Thanks to you. And I'd feel better getting away from you folks until I know what it is I'm facing."

They did not object further. While they prepared for busy days, Taylor placed a call to his secretary's home. "Any word from those visitors of yours?"

"The morning you left for Jacksonville, I called like you asked me to. He said I'd be hearing from them. But I never did. So I called again last night. The phone was disconnected. I checked with the phone company. The number belonged to a cell phone."

"You've done great, Allison."

She breathed in the manner of one releasing a breath she had been holding for days. "I've been so worried."

"Everything is okay."

"Who were they?"

"I'm working on that."

"What do I do with the money?"

"Take a vacation."

"I can't—"

"Take your child and go away. Type out a memo from me to you, instructing you to take some time off, you've been working too hard, the strain from the merger, you know what to say. And sign my name."

"Something's terribly wrong, isn't it?"

"I'm okay. But I don't want to have to worry about you, do you see?"

Taylor hung up the phone with the sense of severing yet another cord tying him to the home he had fashioned for himself. He endured Ruth's inspection and a change of dressings, thanked his friends the best he could, then entered the sullen summer heat.

St. Augustine was marginally hotter than Annapolis and a trace more humid. But the air hung heavier here, as though centuries of semitropical weather carried its own weight. Taylor stopped by a tourist shop at the old town's border and bought a pair of sandals, shorts, and a T-shirt advertising

Augustine's Menéndez Day Festival. He rolled up John's castoffs and put them in the shopping bag. He meandered the streets, walking very slowly, favoring his throbbing leg. It was almost certain no one had tracked him to the home and was following now. But after the previous night Taylor was taking no chances.

He sat in a shaded alcove opposite the hotel and watched the entrance for almost half an hour. Finally a bus too large to make it into the covered alcove halted in front of him and disgorged a bevy of tourists dressed just like himself. Taylor eased into the middle of the crowd and limped across the street and into safety.

He showered a second time, as though hoping to scrub away the previous night and the remaining tremors. He replaced the bandages with extras Ruth had given him, then stretched out on the bed.

He awoke two hours later stiff and sore, as though only now when he was well removed from the danger would his body admit to being hurt.

He slipped out of the hotel's rear entrance and walked down to the Matanzas Inlet Restaurant, a haunt of his father's generation. *Matanzas* meant slaughter in some ancient form of Spanish. The inlet bearing the same name was where Spanish defenders had slaughtered a horde of invading Huguenots. The restaurant attempted to do the same with its brand of Minorcan cuisine. Taylor ordered a bowl of full-strength *perlough,* a native stew of tomatoes, sausages, pilau rice, datil peppers, and whatever vegetables were fresh from market that day. Datil peppers were a native variety that made jalapeño taste like snow cone flavoring. While he waited for his meal, Taylor cleared his nostrils in the traditional manner, sprinkling datil pepper sauce on cream cheese spread over a piece of thick local bread. He ate three such fireballs and drained two pitchers of lemonade before his stew arrived. Minorcan sausage was made from equal parts meat, onion, green pepper, fennel seeds, and datil pepper. They were pickled in vinegar then either boiled or smoked. The natives called them smoke bombs, and for good reason. By the time Taylor left the restaurant, his sweat glands were on overdrive. He felt purged of almost every ounce of fear he'd carried from the night.

The fire in his belly granted his thoughts a special clarity. Taylor held to narrow lanes as he crossed the city's heart, recalling earlier times with a lucidity that made every memory stand out as clearly as etched gold. He remembered walking these very streets, his own hand lost in the hard assuredness of his father's.

Taylor's father had been a great man. Everybody said so. Years after his death, Taylor was still known as Miles Knox's boy, as though being claimed by a man years in the grave granted him entry into a special league. Miles had earned his living as a plumber. Taylor remembered him as a man fierce in all he did. Miles Knox shone with a turbulent ardor. His smile was blinding. Twenty years after his old man's funeral, Taylor could still remember how thrilling it was to watch him grin. A world of anticipation and magnetism went into that simple act, in a way that charmed everyone within reach.

Taylor's newfound clarity was a two-edged sword. As he walked the brick-lined lanes, Taylor found other memories rising unbidden. Of a man who did not always come home when he should. Of odors drifting in the air when he did arrive, sweet odors that somehow had made the little boy sick to his belly. Not the odors, exactly, but rather how they made his mother weep. Miles Knox would stand abject and contrite before his wife, waiting for the storm to pass. His mother was not a fighter. She loved the wayward man too much to leave him. When Miles had aimed his special allure at someone else, she would become hollowed by her pain, defenseless in her determination to hold fast. Then Miles had left them permanently, felled by cancer that ate him from the inside out, saving his gleam and his smile for the last bite.

Taylor slipped through the shadows of an empty street and recalled the anger he had felt, nine years old and forced to stand and watch the hero of his early years sink into the ground. After they had laid Miles Knox to rest, Taylor had gone totally wild. Totally.

Taylor stole into a cool alcove across from the college's environmental science building and studied the terrain. The streets were baking and quiet, but he could see figures moving about inside the lab. He thought he heard his father's voice drift through the dusty air, calling to him. Despite the heat, Taylor found himself shivering. It seemed as though he had been hearing that unspoken voice his entire life, leading him along a road not of his own choosing.

"Can I help you?"

He spun around to face a young man in a lab coat. "I was looking for Dr. Preston."

The man squinted against the heat. "Well, you sure won't find him out here."

Taylor climbed the rear stairs and entered the manufactured coolness. "I didn't want to bother anybody."

"Just stay here a second. I'll see if he's available. What did you say your name was?"

"Taylor Knox. I'm with Revell."

"Oh. Right. Sure. Hang on a second."

The professor could have been drawn from Taylor's own lab team. He was balding and egg-shaped and utterly unconcerned with his physical appearance. He wore a pair of reading glasses on a loop around his neck, a starched lab coat, and rubber slip-ons to avoid static electricity. "You're from Revell?"

"Yes sir. Taylor Knox."

"I can't tell you anything more than I did the other gentlemen. I have no idea where Kirra Revell has gone."

"I understand." He followed the professor down the side

hallway into a cluttered office whose interior window over-looked a busy lab. "Nice place."

"Paid for in large part by your company. Believe me, if I knew where she was, I would be delighted to help out. Coffee?"

"I'm fine, thanks. Can you tell me what Kirra was working on?"

"A rather interesting issue." He waved Taylor into the one seat not piled high with papers and journals. "She was not a scientist."

"She was doing honors studies in local history. Isn't that right?"

"Exactly. She came to me and asked for help with one aspect of her project. Naturally I would not dream of refusing any request from Revell. But what she had was quite fascinat-ing. And highly original." He sprang from his seat, pulled open an overcrammed filing cabinet, fished out a file. "Can I ask what you do for Revell?"

"I run an ops team looking at potential new eye medications."

"So you're not a biochemist."

"No. Sorry. Numbers are my game."

"Then this won't mean any more to you than it did to the last batch they sent."

"Can you tell me about them?"

"Two men. One was a giant. The other I don't recall. A beard, I think. They said they were detectives."

"You told them about Kirra's studies?"

"Yes, but they weren't particularly interested. Just wanted to know where she might have gone, asked a number of highly repetitive questions, and finally left." He returned to his seat, flipped open the chart, and was soon lost in the data.

Taylor gave him a moment. "Dr. Preston."

"Eh, yes?"

"Could you tell me what Kirra was researching?"

"Well, certainly, I mean, what I know of it. She came to me with two items for study. One was a local plant, *Gincava gravis*. Do you know it?"

"Sorry."

"Indigenous species, grows mostly in the interior hills between here and Gainesville. Found nowhere else to our knowledge. She asked me to run a compound analysis. Several, in fact. Apparently, she had found documents suggesting that it had been used as a healing compound by the early Minorcans." His gaze returned to the data. "Nothing of significance in the flower or leaves. But one particular composite within the root system was quite new. We are actually thinking of running a series of tests on it ourselves."

"You said she brought you two plants?"

"The second item was not a plant. Not a plant at all. An artifact. A clay jar that looked quite old. Centuries. She asked me to test the residue."

"And?"

"I have no idea. It was unlike anything we have seen before. Except that it did bear a faint resemblance to the composite found within the roots of the *Gincava gravis*. Which is astonishing."

"Astonishing how?"

"Think about it, man. She identified a medicinal compound from the earliest settlers, perhaps something brought over from Europe. Then she traced how these early healers sought out a local plant that contained a similar sort of compound. This is groundbreaking research. I urged her to write it up. I would present it to a top journal for publication."

"But what does the compound do?"

"Couldn't tell you. Wouldn't even want to hazard a guess. Finding the answer to that would take a great deal of further research. Years. I told her it would make for a fascinating doctorate. One I would be happy to help sponsor."

"Where did she come across the jar?"

"A private collection. I recall her mentioning something about one of the older establishments in the area." He waved the question aside. "It was perfectly in her right to maintain confidentiality while she prepared for publication."

Taylor started to rise, then was halted by a further thought. "What if she found documents that said what the compound had been used for?"

"That would speed things up, certainly. But you don't understand the significance here. More than likely, modern science has already isolated a new compound that does the job better than this old elixir, whatever it was. What is fascinating is that healers of old actually thought enough of this treatment to identify something *here* that worked like what they had *there*. Do you see?"

"I think so."

"This suggests a remarkable degree of scientific study, of testing any number of compounds on patients and themselves until they finally came up with a substitute." The thought was so exciting the professor was unable to remain in his chair. "Think about it, man. What we are seeing is the birth of our nation's pharmaceutical heritage. This might even be the earliest known example of indigenous herbs being adapted for healing by Europeans in the New World."

"Thank you for your time."

"When you find her, tell her she must return and complete this work. Tell her it is a groundbreaking discovery. Groundbreaking."

TAYLOR WAITED UNTIL DARK, THEN ARRIVED AT HIS mother's house via the back route. The fences were more rickety than he remembered, or perhaps he had simply grown more awkward with age and injury. An old hound whose name he did not recall barked once, then smelled his hand and whined in recognition. Obviously the dog's memory was better than his own.

The key was under the same flowerpot. The kitchen door still had to be lifted over the bulge in the linoleum. The odors assaulted him even before he entered the house. He smelled oil-based paints and turpentine and wood smoke and soap. It was the clearest memory of his childhood, these smells.

Taylor was halted by the photograph over the kitchen sink. He had the same picture on his mantel. He and his father were standing on a coulee west of town, their flat-bottomed skiff filled with bass and gear. His father bore a smile so grand it shone in the faint light. Here was a man who could do anything, go anywhere, be forgiven of any failing. Even imparting to his son habits that had destroyed the one relationship he ever wanted to see last.

"Taylor?"

"Hello, Ma."

She came into the kitchen wearing her painting smock, her face and hands decorated by the day's work. "Why didn't you call, son? I haven't got a thing in the house for you to eat."

He hugged her. "I'm not hungry."

"Of course you are. Big strapping boy like you." She moved back far enough to see the bandages. "What on earth have you done to yourself?"

"I scraped my head. It's nothing. How are you?"

"Fine. How else should I be?" She headed for the front room. "Let me just clean up and I'll put something on the stove."

"No thanks, really." The front parlor had been turned into her studio. Taylor's mother had adapted to a hazardous world by pretending. She had a reputation through five states, painting portraits of what wasn't necessarily there. All her subjects were happy. All her painted children shone with the joy of new life. All her families clung together in blissful harmony.

Her easel held a yard-wide portrait of a young couple holding twin infants who had captured enough sunlight to illuminate the room. "That's real nice, Ma."

"It'll do." Her own smile was a somewhat twisted affair, as though the ends of her mouth could not quite release themselves from invisible weights. "Pays the rent."

He watched her use the rag to clean first her brushes and then her hands. He finally spoke because waiting made it no easier. "Ma, I've got to ask you to do something for me."

His tone was enough to freeze her up tight.

"I need you to pack up some things and go stay with Ada for a few days. Not long. A week max."

Taylor expected a serious argument. His mother loved the old place, such that anything he tried to do around the house—be it paint the exterior, fix the sagging front porch, or buy a new fridge—provoked serious dissent. But his mother surprised him by merely asking softly, "Is it a woman?"

"No, Ma."

"You got some girl in trouble. Her family's coming after you."

The way she said it, as a statement drawn from her own shadows, struck him as hard as waking up inside the dungeon. "Did that happen to Pop?"

"We're talking about you, not your father."

As far as Taylor was aware, his mother did not possess a sharp edge to her tongue. But he caught the edge to her words, sure enough. "It's not a woman. Truth, Ma. I'm involved in an investigation at work. The company's being acquired. It's very complicated. A lot of people's jobs are on the line here."

She greeted the news as she did all the darkness in her life, quietly and with eyes wide open. "Now somebody's after you?"

"I can't be certain. But it'd make me sleep a lot better if I knew you were safe. Please, Ma."

She touched his head with turpentine-drenched fingers. "Did they do that to you?"

"Not exactly."

She opened her mouth as if to object. But something she saw in his face changed her mind. She merely sighed and said, "I'll be ready in fifteen minutes."

chapter 6

TAYLOR DROPPED HIS MOTHER OFF AT ADA'S. HE
could not say which was worse—his mother's quiet resigna-
tion or Ada's silent glare.

He drove along the river to the Vilano Bridge and crossed
to the northern barrier island. He passed through Vilano Beach
and took Highway A1A north. Soon he entered the dark and
empty reaches of Guana River State Park. Taylor rolled down
all four windows of his rental car and let the memories wash
in with the warm night breeze. Guana Park had been one of

their favorite meeting places. He had always kept a blanket in his pickup. Kirra would go anywhere he wanted, and she was not a woman who expected to be entertained. She could lie in his arms for hours, content to watch the stars and listen to the ocean's orchestration. That had been a hard lesson for him to learn. At first Taylor had felt challenged to measure up to the ritzy parties he had witnessed on board the floating palace. But Kirra slipped off her wealth as easily as she did her sandals. All she wanted was him, she had whispered in a voice drawn from rushing waves and moonlight.

Taylor pulled the car to the side of the road. He pressed his fists against his eyeballs and fought down the flames of castoff memories. He should have never come back. There was no way to make this warped way straight, or heal these wounds. Taylor punched the wheel. The universe was riven. The course of everyone's life was permanently distorted.

A car roared by him, trailing faint tendrils of laughter and music. Taylor opened his eyes when the sound faded away. The night was empty of all but the heat and the sea breeze. He heaved his aching chest around a sigh. He put the car into gear and headed north.

Sawgrass was a community designed by people who didn't care how much it cost to do exactly what they wanted. It was their attempt to remake the seaside world as they saw fit. An undeveloped lot in Sawgrass went for a million and change. Zoning was so restricted their one McDonald's was housed in a red-brick palace whose golden arches were only three feet high and solid bronze. Taylor parked in a shopping mall done up as a pristine Italian village. He entered the development as he always had for Kirra—over the wall by the seventeenth green.

He tracked around the bordering pines, studying the Revell manor as he would enemy terrain. The house was Provençal in design, with tall dormer windows peeking from the roof of pale tiles. Taylor waited for a security golf cart to meander by, then slipped through the groomed hedges and approached the house. He spied Amanda and her father seated in the living room, talking earnestly with a man he did not recognize. The stranger wore a priest's dark suit and collar. Father and daughter were leaning forward in tight unison. Taylor felt a moment's sympathy for the vicar and the pressure he was enduring.

He climbed the massive live oak, his feet treading along the uppermost branch as he would a familiar path. He slipped over Kirra's balcony and found the key where she had always left it for him. Silently he let himself into her room. He crossed the carpet, hating how the place smelled of Kirra and his own bitter regrets.

He opened the bedroom door and checked the empty hallway. He knew this house so very well, particularly in secret. He slipped down the darkened stairwell, recalling other nights when she would hang on his arm and giggle over the senseless risks they took. Taylor walked down the rear hall and took the last door before the kitchen. The library's lights were on. The home office was precisely as he remembered, the only change a huge aerial photograph of the company's sailing yacht winning some international competition. It hung behind the desk, a place formerly reserved for a portrait of Kirra's mother. The desk was piled high with papers and files bearing the Revell corporate logo. Taylor padded across the Persian carpet and stood looking out the French doors at the night. Kirra's fragrance seemed to have followed him in here, which was impossible. She had always hated this room.

"What are you doing here?"

"Waiting for you." Taylor turned to face an irate Amanda. "We need to talk."

"I have a guest."

"Five minutes."

Carefully she shut the door behind her. "You were supposed to call me last night!"

"I got held up."

Without taking her eyes from him, she crossed to her desk. "Explain."

"You first. Who is after Kirra, Amanda?"

"If I knew that, I'd know where to look for her."

"You've got to have some idea."

"A competitor, maybe. Somebody out to profit from her absence."

"Don't expect me to believe she's become involved in the family company."

"Of course not." Amanda seated herself behind the massive African stinkwood desk. "But you see for yourself how distracted we've become by all this. It would suit a lot of people to know we've taken our eye off the ball."

"Give me a for instance."

"I can't, not with any certainty." Amanda appeared to be genuinely confused by this prospect. "I spend the better part of every night pondering the same question."

"Your goons didn't turn up anything?"

"If they had, you think I'd have asked for your help?" Amanda reached behind the desk and hefted a briefcase of whitened steel. "At least your appearance saves me the need to arrange a handover. Here, take it."

He walked over, snapped the locks, found himself staring at a pile of cash.

"A hundred thousand dollars. Go where you need, buy who you have to. Just bring my sister home."

Taylor's mind was hit by too many conflicting questions. The one that came out was what had carried him this far. "She really asked for me?"

"We've received one message from her. If you want to find me, send Taylor. Nothing else."

"You know she's had a history of running away."

"Not since she got into her religion kick. Besides, this time is different." Amanda let that one hang between them, then finished, "Here's your chance to succeed where you last failed, sport. Don't blow this one. She *needs* you."

"Like you would know. Like you ever understood Kirra."

"Oh, and you're the expert now?"

He made a process of shutting the case and closing the locks. "Back up to when she and I broke up."

"What about it?"

"I want you to admit to putting detectives on my tail."

Amanda sneered as if she had spent years preparing her response. "Was I the one who slept with that peroxided tramp?"

"Answer the question, Amanda!"

"Why should I?" Matching his tone lifted her from the chair. "You want to play inquisitor, how about trying a little of your own medicine? Who was the one who was unfaithful to my little sister?"

"Only that one time! Or didn't your detectives bother—"

"Oh, spare me! You broke her heart!"

"We weren't together! I hadn't seen her in almost two months! She—"

"Save it for somebody who cares, Taylor! Deal with *reality*. She's *gone*."

The door behind them slammed open. "I should have known."

Jack Revell remained ever the patriarch, even when supported by a walker. The priest stood behind him, holding the old man's elbow, not bothering to hide his curiosity.

Jack pointed one shaking hand at Taylor but directed his anger at his daughter. "I warned you this would happen. You allow scum like this back into our lives, he'll never let go!"

"Leave it alone, Pop." Amanda no longer sounded angry. Only tired. "You know we have no choice."

"Scum!" Jack's entire arm trembled with the rage of ages. "I should have had you shot and salted and mounted for what you did to my daughter! You wounded my family. You shredded every hope of recovering Kirra and bringing her back into the fold!"

"That's not—"

A bullet blasted through the French doors, lodging in the wall between him and Kirra's father. Instinctively, Taylor leaped forward and dragged both Jack Revell and the panicked priest out of the line of fire.

Amanda shrieked and dove behind the desk as a multitude of guns opened up. Both sets of French doors shattered. Glass and wall plaster fell like arid rain.

Taylor heaved Jack Revell back down the hallway. The old man was still raging over Taylor's audacity in doing anything other than what Jack Revell ordered him to do. The priest lay with his hands over his head, his jacket now white with dust.

The shooting halted. Amanda used that instant to crawl to the hall's relative safety, dragging the briefcase with her. She shared her father's rage, only hers was aimed at the attackers. "How *dare* they do this!"

"You see?" Jack's voice was hoarse from the dust and the strain, but his rage at Taylor was unabated. "This is his fault! He wasn't satisfied with—"

"Quiet!" Amanda rammed the briefcase into Taylor's arms. "Go!"

"My car is five blocks from here." He heard sirens in the distance. "Let's wait for the police."

"No!"

"It'll be safer for everybody, Amanda."

"You can't be seen! They can't know you're looking!"

Taylor tried to say they already knew, but Amanda was not in listening mode. She shoved a set of keys at him. "Take my car from the garage! Get the priest out of here! *Run!*"

chapter 7

NATURALLY, AMANDA'S CAR WAS THE MOST EXPEN-
sive Porsche on the road, a silver convertible Carrera Turbo. It
was parked facing out with the top down. With the priest cow-
ering in the passenger seat beside him, Taylor punched buttons
all over the dash until the garage door started grinding up. He hit
the starter. The noise exploded around them like audible flames.

Taylor blasted out of the house like a rocket impatient to
leave the pad. He roared down the lane and did a four-point
skid into the main road. He hit a hundred in second gear

while he was still approaching the guard station. The security cop on night duty must have recognized both the car and the manner of driving, because the barrier bounced up like it was afraid. The cop stepped from the brick house to shout something about gunfire, but Taylor could not risk raising one hand in a wave. The car was that fierce.

He blasted out of Sawgrass and aimed south. The night whipped about them in fragrances of frangipani and salt. Fifteen minutes into the screaming flight, he realized that their speed alone was enough to get him locked up forever. He slowed to a relatively sane seventy-five. The motor seemed to grumble at being reined back. Only then did Taylor realize that his entire body was trembling.

He pulled off the road, turned off the motor, and got out of the car. He looked down at his passenger. The priest had neither moved nor spoken. "Are you hit?"

"They said she was in danger." The priest was neither young nor old, his face a series of taut creases, his features even, his dark hair framed with silver flecks. "I had no idea."

"Excuse me?"

He turned his face upward. A passing car reflected upon clear gray eyes. "You are Taylor Knox."

Then it hit him. "Father Pellecier?"

"It seems we have both been informed of the other's existence." The father smiled. "I hope they spoke more favorably of me than they did of you."

"They didn't tell me a thing. Ada Folley suggested . . . never mind." He slid back into the car. "Do you know where Kirra is?"

"Let me see if I understand this correctly." He had a professor's precise way of speaking. Every word was laid in place with ecumenical precision. "Are you not the young man responsible for crushing my favorite student's heart?"

Taylor restarted the motor and pulled into the night.

"So now I am supposed to trust you with information I have refused to give her own family. Which is not much, I hasten to add. But what I have was shared in confidence."

Taylor raised his voice against the wind. "You saw the gunfire. I don't need to tell you the danger she may be facing."

When the priest did not respond, Taylor shot him a glance. The man watched him intently. Waiting.

"I'm going to find her and make it right."

"Are you."

He caught the tone. "I can fix things between us."

"Can you."

"We broke up. It happens. We can get back together. She needs me."

But the father merely observed him, his gaze holding all the answer Taylor needed. Or deserved. He slowed down to where the motor was merely a constant rumble. "If I were in your place, I wouldn't trust me either."

The father visibly relaxed. "Honesty. Excellent. After what we have just been through, I can think of nothing more welcome. Do you have any idea who might have been behind the attack on the Revell house?"

"No. Not why, not who. All I can say for certain is that it wasn't the first." He related what had happened to him at the Spanish fortress. "Amanda thinks it could be a competitor wanting to take her eye off the work at hand."

"You disagree?"

"Kirra ran away from something. She chose not to tell her family where she was headed. That sounds like more than a competitor's scare tactics at work."

"I agree." Pellecier scrunched into his seat, pondering the dark night. "You sound to me like a man who is still in love." He gave Taylor a moment to respond, then finished the thought. "Yet you broke her heart."

"It isn't as straightforward as you probably heard."

"You argued over her faith and your lack." It was not a question. "She has talked of you quite a lot, you see. I suppose it was her way of ridding herself of what was no longer, of preparing for life with another. But sometimes I wondered."

The internal pressure made Taylor fight for the breath to say, "Wondered about what?"

"Whether it was her way of keeping your memory alive. She seemed to be searching for some way to forgive the unforgivable."

"What did you tell her?"

The priest was a long time in replying. "Very little of any use, I am afraid."

It no longer mattered that he spoke to a total stranger. Or that the words scalded his throat as they emerged. "You know how I became certain her faith was real? Kirra found a desire to do what didn't come easy. Or naturally. She wanted to be more than she was. She wanted to be *better*. A better person, a better lover . . ."

Father Pellecier had turned slightly in his seat so that he could study Taylor fully. The man seemed to radiate an intensity, one so great Taylor found himself able to speak thoughts he had scarcely formed inside himself. Taylor continued. "My father ran around. I've known it all my life. But I never *thought* about it until this trip. I remember how he used to slip in the back door sometimes, like an old tomcat who wanted to pretend he hadn't just vanished on us for a night or a weekend. Once he was gone for a whole week. Then he'd slip back in, and he'd pretend hard as he could that nothing was wrong. He was good looking and he had a great smile and everybody liked him. That's really all I know about him. Even now people smile when they talk about him. They smile at me and they say I'm just like him. And they wait for me to smile back."

Father Pellecier responded with the voice of a professional listener, void of judgment, focused both on what was said and on what could never be spoken aloud. "You loved him very much."

"Yeah. He was a great dad. When he was around." Up ahead glimmered the lights of Vilano Beach. Taylor released his grip on the wheel long enough to swipe at his face. "The thing is, I *am* just like him. I wanted the easy times with Kirra. I wanted the goodness she brought to me, but I didn't want to change. I wanted to be just exactly what I wanted to be, and have that be enough." He knew he was babbling. He was talking secrets he had never really confessed to himself, and he didn't *care*. "Then things got bad. She wanted what I wasn't able to give her. I wanted . . ."

"You wanted a woman of the world." He offered the words so calmly Taylor was able to accept them. "You wanted her on your terms."

"Yeah. I guess that's . . . anyway, she wouldn't, you know. So I figured, what the hey, we're in love, she's as good as anybody I'll ever meet, better than I deserve, that's for sure. So let's get married. I thought, what more could I do?"

Pellecier gripped the dash as Taylor took the turn and started across the bridge toward the mainland. The lights overhead flashed across them, illuminating far more than the interior of Amanda's car. "And she turned you down," the priest said.

"Flat. Wouldn't even talk about it."

"Of course. How could she agree to marry someone who refused to share the most important thing in her life?"

"Funny. I thought I was the most important thing."

"Was she that to you?"

"Sure. Absolutely."

"So why was it, I wonder, that you could not accept change? You yourself have said you loved this woman. She was vital to your existence. Is that not what you said?" Pellecier leaned in close. "Yet you would not change. That is interesting, yes? Could it perhaps be that something else was *more* important? Something you did not want to admit even to yourself?"

Tourists taking advantage of night's relative cool filled the walks up ahead. Taylor spun the car in a tight corner, pulling into the lot behind the fortress. He cut the motor and focused upon the priest. He said the words, but even before they were spoken he recognized how he used them as a shield. What was worse, he knew he had done it many times before. "I loved Kirra."

"Of course you did. No one is doubting that. But it was a *flawed* love."

He tried for scorn but could not quite swing it. "You're saying there's perfection in this world?"

The priest was clearly disappointed with his response. "In this world, yes. *Of* this world, no." Then he waited.

Taylor saw in the man's eyes that he was being offered a last chance to justify the gift of trust. "Sir, I don't know what it is you want me to say. But I can tell you this. The longer I work on this, the more certain I become that I'm not doing this for myself. Not anymore."

Father Pellecier climbed from the car. He inspected Taylor so long he feared the man would deny him any hope of a lead, simply turn and walk away. Instead the priest said, "I became friends with Kirra during her search of our earliest records. The first settlers were by and large a wealthy lot, granted land titles by the Spanish royalty. The Minorcans arrived about a century later, indentured slaves originally brought to the area around what is now New Smyrna. Ah, I see you did not know that. Yes. But that settlement failed, and the survivors migrated north. They were lured by offers of freedom and land in return for years of bonded servitude. For most it was the best chance they had ever known.

"Were it not for a band of my brethren, the lore of these earliest Europeans would have long been lost. What little we have has survived a multitude of wars, pestilence, starvation, and three hundred years of callous indifference. Only in the past few years have we received funding to begin the research and translation."

"Which came from the Revell family's foundation," Taylor guessed. "Which is why you agreed to see them tonight."

Father Pellecier fanned vaguely at the night. He would give Taylor only what he chose. "Kirra volunteered to aid in the cataloging process, in return for unrestricted access to all the newly translated documents. I cannot tell you precisely what she was looking for, because I did not choose to ask her myself."

"I know it had to do with early American herbal remedies and their relationship to medications used in Europe."

"Kirra discovered the existence of a foundation in Europe studying such early remedies. They have become a gathering point for documents long forgotten and thought lost forever." Then the priest stopped.

The night was too filled with the rawness of Taylor's heart's exposure to do more than beg. "A name, Father. Give me a name."

The priest stared down at Taylor, his gaze as shimmering and unreadable as star-dashed waters. "She turned to faith because of you, my son."

The notion was so preposterous Taylor shouted his rejection. "That is totally absurd!"

"It is the absolute truth."

"It can't be. Didn't you hear a thing I just said?"

"I have heard everything you spoke and more."

"Kirra's religion drove us apart!"

"Perhaps." The priest only grew more placid in the face of Taylor's ire. More certain of his course. "But it was a risk she chose to take out of her love for you."

"That's insane!"

"No, my son. It was love at its most revealing. Kirra saw into your heart of hearts. She recognized the pain and the rage you carry. And she realized she could not heal these wounds on her own."

Father Pellecier leaned upon the Porsche's door and clubbed

Taylor with his whispers. "She took the step into faith not for herself. She was too strong and willful to ever admit to such a need. She did it for *you*. She wanted so much to see you truly healed. She came to the Cross, made broken and alone by her love. Then she tried to show you the way. And how did you respond?"

Taylor's mouth worked. But the sounds would not come.

"Go to Iona," Father Pellecier continued, spelling out the name. "Iona is an island off the western coast of Scotland. On it you will find an ecumenical monastery. That word is new to you, yes? Ecumenical means that it holds to no particular denomination. All seekers are welcome, so long as their purpose is true. Ask for Brother Jonah."

The priest stepped away from the car and signed the cross into the night between them. "Go with God, my son. I will pray that you are successful in all your quests, and for all the right reasons. And when you find her, I pray that she says we both took the proper course this night."

IN AN EARLIER AND MORE LIGHTHEARTED AGE,
Taylor might have described the gift of a new Porsche Cabrio
and a hundred thousand dollars as his idea of heaven.

But this particular night he felt a billion years old, petrified
to emotionless and laughterless stone. He kept the top down
as he raced for Orlando. He tried several radio stations, but
neither rock nor jazz nor tunes from somebody else's past
could dispel the interior fog. So he made do with the wind and
his own tumbling thoughts.

At two in the morning he stopped for gas and an energy drink. He blasted out of the station and hit 120 on the interstate entrance ramp. Then he slowed, finally accepting that he could not outrun his thoughts any more than he could flee his own skin.

The issue was pure, unfettered, male-driven pride.

The thought shouted at him from all sides. The motor's roar and the wind's rush were reformed to echo what he could not escape. He had refused to change, just as the priest had said. Oh yes. Every time Kirra had spoken or pleaded or argued, seeking for him to do what he would rather avoid, this had been his answer: He had raised the shield of arrogance and refused to budge. As though being a man was enough answer. As though he had been born perfect. As though he had the answer to anything.

Taylor arrived at Orlando's international airport an hour before dawn. He took an early breakfast at an all-night Denny's, then bought a round-trip first-class ticket for the first flight to London, later that morning. The British Airways ticket agent had never heard of Iona. But anyone purchasing a first-class ticket deserved special service. The agent found Iona on a map, then arranged a connecting flight to Glasgow.

Taylor stopped at the rental car counter and announced that he had abandoned their vehicle at a shopping center in Sawgrass. The woman took pity on his tattered state and was mild in both her condemnation and her warning of charges to come. He then called the Hotel Casa Monica, checked out, and ordered them to store his luggage. Afterward Taylor meandered into the airport's central food court and tanked up on coffee. His entire body felt grainy from the previous two days. Even so, he did not feel a need to sleep as much as a desire to put even more miles between himself and all he had just been forced to confront.

At nine he called the office and was less than pleased to hear Allison's voice answer the phone. "What are you doing here?"

"Just a second." She set down the phone, then returned. "Where are you?"

"Allison, shutting the door won't do us any good if they've bugged your office."

"They're gone. I told you that. The phone number they gave me was disconnected."

"They're not gone. Believe me. They've just relocated."

"Taylor, I've got a thousand better ways to spend money than on a vacation I can't afford."

He stared at the airport world sweeping by his phone. "I need to ask you something."

"So ask."

"When exactly did the goon drop by your office and ask you to spy on me?"

Her guarded tone answered his question before the words were fully formed. "Exactly, oh, six days ago."

"So it was before you invited me to dinner."

Allison had a special edge she showed any man who pestered.

It had the feel of a blade honed from dry ice. She had never turned it on him. Until now. "That's what you think?"

"I'm asking because I have to, Allison. They've tried to kill me."

"Who has?"

"Most likely the same team who popped into your office." When she remained silent, he added, "I've always been completely aboveboard with you. That's what I'm trying to do now."

"I didn't invite you over because of them."

"Why didn't you tell me about the guy showing up when it happened?"

"Because I needed the money. You don't know . . . never mind."

He looked at the silver case nestled between his feet. "I understand."

"You can't possibly."

"You've got a daughter; you've got emergencies. I've been where you are. Lower. And without a kid. I know what it's like to be tempted."

She released a cold torrent of words. "I didn't want to do it. But I had to. So I said yes. Then I couldn't. Which made it even worse. I'd never thought of you like that before. I mean, you're my *boss*. I spent two days and nights arguing with myself. Then I realized I couldn't fight it. So I invited you over for dinner. And you were so *nice*."

He took a long breath. "I believe you."

There was a silence, then, "You've been attacked?"

"Twice."

"But why?"

"I can't say for certain. I'm working on something for the Revell family. I'll tell you about it when I'm back."

"Are you all right?"

"I'm a little tired."

The thaw was only partial. "You sound exhausted."

"Is anything going on I should know about?"

"Gowers has been down here every single day."

"What?"

"Sometimes twice. Asking about you. Most days he shows up here alone. He pops in, takes a quick look around, asks for you, then whoosh, he's gone again."

The company president never entered *any* lab without his aides, for fear of being cornered and hounded over funding. "That doesn't make any sense."

"Then yesterday he showed up in a real rage. We're talking one inch from detonation. He said something about the merger being put on hold. He made it sound like it was your fault. Like Revell was only going through with the deal if you delivered."

"I'm missing something here."

"What do you want me to do?"

He rubbed around the bandaged spot on his head. Taylor had no choice but to trust her. At least for now. "I need you to check out Revell. Try and discover what new products they're working on. Can you do that and not have it be traced back?"

"I suppose so." Thinking as she spoke. "I'll get our resident techies to check for me."

"Perfect." The lab rats would cross burning coals in their bare feet if she asked.

"What should I tell them to look for?"

"I need to know what's new in the corporate pipeline."

"That's not much to go on."

"That's all I have." If he rubbed his face any harder, he'd take off skin. But the fatigue refused to relinquish its hold. "I'll call you when I arrive."

"Where are you going?"

"I better not say."

"Taylor—"

"It'll be a day or so before I make contact. Take care, Allison. And thanks."

TAYLOR FIRST STOPPED BY THE AIRPORT SHOPS AND bought himself two changes of clothes in garish tourist colors and a nylon duffel. He went back to the Porsche and drove to the first bank whose sign he spotted. He went straight to the duty manager and said he wanted to open an account with cash. The contents of his briefcase was good for a couple of slow blinks. The manager then announced that any cash deposit of more than ten thousand dollars had to be registered with the FDIC. Taylor gave his address care of Amanda Revell, CEO of the Revell Corporation, laying a clear paper trail. The banker accepted this stamp of legality with relief and helped him stack the bills.

Taylor said he was going to England on business for the company and asked how much he could safely carry with him. The banker was too busy keeping score to even look up. England had no limits on cash imports, he replied. So Taylor decided to keep five thousand in cash and fifteen in traveler's checks. Why so much, he could not say. Maybe because he'd never had that sort of the ready before. He put another ten thousand into a FedEx envelope and addressed it to Allison. He accepted the banker's handshake and headed back to the airport.

He slept the entire way across the Atlantic. The flight attendant had kept his meal hot, so he dined on overdry steak and wilted vegetables as they prepared for landing. All he saw of London's Gatwick Airport was a sofa in the first-class lounge. Two and a half hours later an agent shook him awake and said he was about to miss his connecting flight. He stumbled through Gatwick, halting only long enough to change money at one of the exchange booths.

In Glasgow, Taylor took a room at the airport hotel, showered for almost an hour and a half, and collapsed across his bed. He awoke four hours later, ordered a massive room-service meal, and tried to ignore how his eyes still felt gritty from the journey and some very long days.

He took a taxi to the downtown train station and found himself totally defeated by the ticket master's accent. The man clearly understood where Taylor wanted to go, but what he said in reply might as well have been in Romanian. Finally the ticket agent motioned in universal sign language. Taylor slipped through a bundle of bills. The man punched out a ticket and passed it back with the change. Most of the people in line behind Taylor were enjoying the show. A woman took him by the arm and led him down to the proper track. With a mother's patience she made him understand that the name on his ticket, Oban, was as close as the train would come to his destination. She waved his train out of the station, clearly worried over this bedraggled American with the bandaged head.

The day was gray, the wind cold, the scenery dismal. Clay chimneys shaped like upside-down pots emerged from steep slate roofs. They emitted thin streams of smoke that rose to join the lowering sky. The streets were clogged with early morning traffic. The air tasted of diesel fumes and coming rain. Taylor shivered in his Florida-bought clothes and hunkered down in his seat. People crowded the sidewalks with blank faces. They all seemed to wear clothes as gray as the day. The houses were brick and jammed tight against one another. Little flecks of carefully tended green formed rear gardens scarcely larger than the window through which he looked.

The sun and summer both seemed a million miles away from this place.

He dozed off, then jerked awake, fearful he had missed his stop. But a man in the passageway found great humor in slowing his speech and yelling overloud that Taylor had an hour yet to go.

Gradually the train emerged from the red-brick city confines. The countryside scenery was craggy and irregular. Steep-sided hills fell into valleys lost to the rain now lashing his window. Villages emerged like gray havens and just as swiftly disappeared. Despite the wet chill, Taylor opened his window and took deep draughts of the morning. The next village was his destination. When Taylor stepped onto the platform, he was greeted by the unmistakable fragrance of open sea.

He left the station and pointed his face into the wind. The air might be forty degrees colder, the village utterly alien. But he was ocean born and bred. He knew this was a seaborne storm. Father Pellecier had told him Iona was an island. There had to be both a port and a boat.

Midway down the lane, however, he was halted by an utterly unexpected sight. He pushed through the door and had to laugh out loud.

There were two young men behind the counter. One grinned back and said something utterly incomprehensible.

Taylor asked, "Do you speak English?"

The servers shared a laugh over that. "Aye, that I do. I even speak a passable Yank. What can I do for you?"

"I need some warm clothes." But his gaze remained fastened on the long array of boards stacked down the far wall. "Is there surf around here?"

That drew another laugh. "Fresh caught, are we, Yank?"

"Excuse me?"

"When did your ship get in?"

"I just flew over last night."

"Right. And from the shade of your skin, I'd say it was warmer where you left."

"Florida."

"Flawda. Aye, we've heard of that spot, haven't we, Eric? They even claim to have waves in Flawda. So what's a Flawda man doing in the wilds of Scotland?"

Taylor drew out a new thruster, a three-finned surfboard with the long narrow dimensions required for big waves. "I'm headed for Iona."

"Wrong answer, Flawda. That is, assuming you know what to do with that stick in your hand." The guy was all Scots, right down to his red-gold beard and massive build and mocking tone. He had the windblown features of one blasted by storms far fiercer than those of today. "Know why? Cliffs. Rocks. Currents. Bad place for surfing, Iona."

Taylor started pulling clothes off the racks. "How do I get there?"

"Point your nose into the wind and walk downhill. Boats leave for Mull every other hour."

"But I want to go—"

"To Iona. Aye, I heard you the first time." He spoke with the musical cadence of one addressing a small child. "Take the Caledonian MacBrayne ferry to Craignure on the island of Mull. Cross the island by bus to Fionnphort. Catch the ferry from there to Iona."

"Is all life in Scotland this complicated?"

"Only the things that matter. Here, I'll write it out for you."

"Thanks." All the surf shop's clothes were fashioned for heavy weather. Chain-knit pullovers, fur-lined boots, double-thick sweats, hooded foul-weather gear. Taylor made a pile on the counter. "I don't have enough pounds to pay for this. Do you take dollars?"

"There's a bank down the road; they'll give you a better rate."

"I'm sort of in a hurry."

"Just like a Yank. Sure, we'll be delighted to rob you gently." He made a merry procedure of ringing up the sale. As he watched Taylor stow away his new gear, he offered, "Funny, you don't strike us as one made for the holy orders."

"I'm looking for a friend."

The two Scots exchanged a look and said together, "A lass."

Taylor did not deny it.

"Is she a Yank like yourself, then?"

Taylor's only response was to zip his carryall closed and ask, "How much do I owe you?"

"Sure, now. Nothing wrong with a man who keeps his business close." He handed Taylor his change in sterling. "You get done mixing it up across the waters, stop on by. Should be a nice swell after this blow."

THE FERRY CROSSINGS WERE ELONGATED BY A RUSHING tide and waves compressed within narrow rocky straits. The current sweeping between the mainland port and the first set of islands was strong as a flooded river. The rain fell in heavy sheets. The wind defied Taylor to call the month August.

Iona appeared like a storm cloud too heavy to rise from the sea. Sheer cliffs gray as the sky ignored the booming waves. The craft steamed well clear of the raging backwash, rounded the island's southern tip, and entered a miniature harbor formed by two rocky arms.

The island was craggy and wind-swept and largely desolate. The church rose like a gray stone beacon. A series of stone structures stretched along the headlands facing across the inner waters. They were washed utterly colorless from the day.

As he ascended the road leading up from the harbor, Taylor found a trio of young people trimming rocks and laying stones into a partially completed wall. He asked them if they knew a Brother Jonah.

They shared a quick smirk before the girl replied, "Everybody knows him."

"Can you tell me where I'd find him?"

Her head was bared to the weather, her face streaked with rain and simple good cheer. "Are you sure you're up to it?"

"Excuse me?"

Every word she spoke carried a musical lilt. "Do you not know the man you're after?"

"All I have is a name."

"Then a word to the wise." She accepted the next stone and set it into place. "Head for the kitchen, but don't say anything about his cooking."

"Thanks, I guess."

The kitchen and dining hall occupied a central position among the simple stone structures. Only the church stood out, rising like a man-made cliff from the cluster. Taylor followed the odors of cooking until he stood before an open door and called, "Brother Jonah?"

A voice cried out, "Are you the chef?"

"No."

A burly man bearing a steaming pot in one hand and a ladle in the other stumped into view. "You're absolutely certain you're not my new cook?"

"Sorry."

"Then what good are you?" He glared at Taylor as though expecting open defiance. "I specifically asked God to bring me a cook. The Good Book says He delivers when His servants ask, or has my addled brain mislaid the quotation along with the cooking salt?"

"I couldn't tell you."

"You can't cook and you don't know your Scriptures. Can you read?"

"Yes."

"Well, it's a sad state when I'm forced to admit a man's eyes are his only attribute." He spun away. "What are you standing there in the rain for? Get in here!"

Taylor dropped his carryall by the sink. "Actually, I'm here—"

"I know why you're here. You're here because you're hungry. And it won't do you a bit of good carrying on about your belly when I've burned the roast and I can't see what it says about the sprouts!" He jabbed his ladle at an open book. "Read me what it says I'm supposed to do next."

Taylor stepped to the book. "Where were you?"

"If I knew that I wouldn't need help, now, would I? Go on, step aside, step aside." He muttered his way down the page, then cried, "Blanch? What in heaven's name does it mean to blanch the legumes?"

"I think it's a sort of steaming."

He glared at Taylor. "Did you write this nonsense?"

"Me, what? No!"

"Never mind, you know more than I do." He pointed at a vast pile of greens rising from the sink. "Go on, then. Blanch away."

Taylor decided he was better off doing what he could. He

recalled Ada's movements from many stolen moments in the Revell's kitchen, sought out a metal strainer, filled the largest pot he could find with water, and set it on the stove. He washed the vegetables and set the overstuffed strainer above the heating water.

The kitchen subsided into a rather sullen calm. Brother Jonah had a mild argument with the oven, scolded the meat, whipped the gravy into brown froth, and had nothing nice to say about the potatoes. But he found enough favor in Taylor's actions to refrain from shouting anything further in his direction.

Two hours later, several young people silently entered the kitchen. One of them was the young lady Taylor had seen working on the wall. The newcomers kept as much distance as possible between themselves and Jonah. They gathered plates and glasses and silverware and returned to the dining hall.

During one of the interims when they had the kitchen to themselves, Brother Jonah sidled over, tasted one of the sprouts, and confided, "I positively loathe cooking."

"Really?" Taylor was weary enough to maintain a straight face. "I had no idea."

"Loathe it. Why the good Lord couldn't simply deposit His bounty upon this earth fully cooked is beyond me. But our resident chef is laid up with the croup, and the director-general said serving kitchen duty would do wonders for my soul. Here, why don't you finish preparing the joint." He handed

Taylor his carving knife. "Our director-general is getting old. I fear age has addled his brains."

The roast looked as if it had been attacked with a blunt ax. Taylor decided this was as good a time as any to confess, "I'm actually looking for Kirra Revell."

"Don't saw it so thick; you're not cutting logs. You can't possibly imagine the problems of cooking in robes. Kitchens and robes. Robes and kitchens. Such a bother. I was standing here yesterday when this sullen-looking wasp fell off the window and landed on me. One moment it was on my sleeve. The next, whish. It disappeared. Where did it go? I can only imagine." He forked sliced meat onto a serving tray. "Seven holes I have in this robe. So many for him to choose from. I never did find that wasp."

"Do you know Kirra?"

"I heard you the first time." Jonah poured tureens full of gravy and handed them to the incoming servers. "She said someone might be showing up, asking for her."

"Is she here?"

"Aye, that is the question."

Jonah moved to the far counter where he began mashing potatoes. Taylor knew nothing was to be gained by pushing this man. He finished carving the joint and piled the remaining meat on another serving dish.

The young lady returned, picked up the carved meat, and said softly to Taylor, "Two hours in the place and already the handsome stranger's being called a miracle worker."

"Excuse me?"

She had a dancer's ability to shimmer even when standing still. "You're the first who's managed to last this long in Jonah's company."

Taylor kept his back to the brother. "He's okay."

"That he most definitely is not." She had a musical laugh. "I'm Gabrielle."

Taylor faced her fully to reply, "And I am here looking for a lady."

"That's not what I was asking."

"Yes," Taylor replied. "It was."

"Well then." She picked up the platter and headed for the dining room. "Best hurry or you won't find a thing save crumbs."

But when Taylor wiped his hands and turned around, he found Jonah watching him with something akin to approval. The older man scraped out the remains of his potatoes, handed the bowl to a final server, then waited until the kitchen was theirs alone to say, "Tell me something that would make it proper to trust you."

"I can't and you know it."

He liked that response enough to say, "Kirra is not here."

Taylor nodded. He had already sensed this.

"Was she the only reason you came?"

"Yesterday I thought so." He continued to wipe his hands with the dishtowel. "Now I'm so tired I really couldn't tell you."

"And is your fatigue the only reason for a lack of decent reasons, I wonder?"

The window was pelted with rain fierce as drumbeats. "I don't even know enough to name what it is I'm facing."

"So this could be a quest for yourself as well as for the lady."

He nodded slowly, liking how that sounded, though he could not say why. "Maybe."

Jonah came to stand beside him and watch the storm. "There was no place hit harder by the Great Depression than Scotland, and no place worse off in Scotland than Glasgow. People in these parts had every reason to give up and give in. Many did. But one man by the name of George MacLeod brought a group of unemployed here to Iona. They begged funds from people who had nothing to give. And they rebuilt the abbey you see there. It's almost a thousand years old, this place. Deserted four long centuries, since the days of Henry VIII. You know why MacLeod and his men came?"

"I have no idea."

"MacLeod said they wanted to set an example for the land as a whole. How such dark times can be a chance for great achievements, even the rebuilding of a holy place long lost to ruin."

"I like that."

"Do you now?" He turned to Taylor. "Here's a question for you, then."

"I'm not sure I need any more questions about myself."

"Ah, that's where you're wrong, lad." He might have smiled, but the flicker was so fast it may well have been just a twitch. "MacLeod called Iona a thin place. He meant there was not much separating the earthly from the divine." He reached out, as though ready to pat Taylor's shoulder, then thought better of it. "Come talk with me again when you think you've reached an understanding of the good man's words."

TAYLOR'S ABILITY TO WORK ALONGSIDE BROTHER
Jonah earned him one of the center's last unfilled berths. There
was space for about fifty in the compound. The monastery
offered the only decent housing on the island. Taylor bunked
with four other men in a simple stone chamber. The building
had a slate-tiled roof, narrow storm-sheltered windows, and
no heat. His bunkmates were an odd assortment of young
and old, professional and longtime unemployed. They were
friendly in a reserved sense, speaking little but making him feel

welcome just the same. The entire island held to a quietness that anywhere else might have been unsettling. Here, however, it suited.

The wind blasted and the rain pelted all afternoon. Taylor dozed for a time, then awoke to the sound of a single lonely bell. He followed the others to the abbey and sat through a prayer service, watching and saying nothing.

Everyone worked. There was an unhurried intensity to the place, a quiet acceptance of the people and the weather and a life stripped down to bare bones. People smiled his way, said a few words, but did not press.

Late afternoon he returned unbidden to the kitchen. Brother Jonah accepted him in matter-of-fact gruffness and set him to making a dozen quiches. He had gained the rudiments of cooking from serving in Ada's galley. He neither liked nor disliked the work. At least the kitchen was warm.

By the time the washing up was done, fatigue swept over him in time to the blasting winds. He stumbled into his bunk room and was asleep before his head hit the pillow.

He awoke to a gray and blustery dawn. One man in the opposite bunk snored so loudly it drowned out the wind. But that was not what had disturbed Taylor's sleep. He rose, found pants and shoes, and padded to the bathroom at the end of the long stone hall. Outside, the rain continued to drum its constant Scottish message.

The light was muted, the odors close and cold. Taylor

crossed the courtyard and entered the dark kitchen. The wall clock read a quarter past six. Morning prayers were at seven, breakfast at seven thirty. Nothing was obligatory, but all overnight guests were asked to participate in the community's life.

Taylor began carving slices from the great round loaves and filling the bread baskets. The tasks were similar to kitchen duty among the boat's staff, and relatively mindless. Which was precisely what he wanted. He ignored the bell's muted clang to prayer. He boiled water for three dozen pots of tea and filled the butter trays and set out the breakfast plates. All the while, his mind remained locked on what had driven him from his bed.

Though the image had become clarified only in that instant between sleep and wakefulness, it seemed to Taylor he had been carrying it ever since St. Augustine. A rancid seed had long lain dormant within him, waiting for a time when his mind became fallow. At dawn the image had come to him full blown. Taylor was tempted to call it merely a dream, but the air was too pure here to permit such a lie. Particularly one he would be telling only to himself.

He remembered. Oh yes. It was not a dream, but rather a recollection so vivid he was astonished it had remained dormant this long.

He had been no more than six at the time, pushing a toy car around the backyard. His father had been seated upon the rear stoop, a bottle of something cold wedged between his work boots. Sweating as hard as the bottle, his father had watched Taylor with a bemused expression, as though uncertain what role he should be playing in this simple family theater.

Taylor worked hard at pretending that everything was fine. His father was home from his latest plumbing job; his mother was inside making dinner. But far more than the screen door separated the two adults. Taylor made puttering noises as he drove his toy car through the grass, knowing his father's eyes were on him. Finally he rose from his crouch and went over to sit beside his dad. His father had been away for a night or two or seven, and now was home again. The atmosphere held a sick quality, like an illness that was never spoken of but that was slowly killing whatever good had once resided in their family.

Taylor spun the wheels of his little car and heard his mother step out of the kitchen and into her room at the front of the house. She would stay there, working at her easel, until it was time for the boys to come inside and eat their silent dinner. His father had tipped back the bottle, swallowed, then said to no one in particular, "When you want it, you don't get it. And when you get it, you don't want it."

Taylor had looked up at what to him was the strongest man in the world. "What does that mean, Pop?"

His father had stared at the bottle in his hands. "It's just something my old man used to say."

"Will I understand better when I grow up?"

His father had looked at Taylor then, as sad a man as ever had walked the earth. "I hope not, boy. I surely do hope not."

HE HAD NO IDEA HOW LONG HE STOOD THERE, STARING blindly at a world washed of all color. Nor could he say how long Jonah had been there beside him. The brother wore the same gray chain-link sweater as the previous day, the same frown. He stood with arms crossed, watching Taylor with an air that said he was willing to stand there all day.

Taylor said simply, "I'm not ready for this."

"Oh, and you think anyone ever is?" He addressed a server Taylor had not even noticed. "Grab the vittles and be gone with you." Then he returned his attention to Taylor. "God's first task is to confront us with a very simple fact. We can't do this on our own. But it's not pleasant. Nor is it meant to be."

"I probably should leave here."

"And go where, pray tell? Back to a life busy enough you don't need to ever look at the mistakes you carry?" He gave Taylor a chance to object, then continued, "People hear about how Iona is a thin realm. How heaven is near to this place. So they show up full of expectations. How they'll be filled with the Spirit and go off dancing across the waves. And maybe it happens, to the few who are far more perfect than you or I. But that's not our lot. We're the ones who think we're strong, who've always managed well enough on our own, thank you very much. What do you suppose we find here?"

Taylor shook his head. He did not have the strength to guess.

"We come face to face with our own *lack*. The needs we try so hard to ignore. The wants we bury beneath the lies of this world."

Taylor fought against the internal tumult and managed to frame the words, "She hurt me. I hurt her back. I thought I could justify it and forget it. But I can't."

Impatiently Jonah waved away his words. "That's not what we're on about here. That is *past*. This is *now*. The question is not about making amends. The question is how best to prepare for *this day*. If you were to have the chance to do it all over again, would you do any better in the here and now?"

Taylor reached out and traced a raindrop down the window. Just as he had done with tears upon Kirra's face. And not just once. He had not wounded her just the one time. He held on to that particular memory because it had been the *last* time.

"There. You see? Lad, there's a passage in the Scriptures that talks about the fruits of this world versus the fruits of the Spirit. It's a simple enough chore to translate that into the fruits of an earthly relationship. Do you see what I'm going on about here? No, of course you don't. How could you, since you've never seen a need to read God's Word? Listen to me, then. So long as your eyes remain set upon the things of this world, your acts will lead to earthbound results." He counted the items on stubby fingers. "Guilt, remorse, painful reflection, sullenness, bitterness, self-hatred, cynicism, weariness, repetition of past mistakes . . . How am I doing so far?"

Taylor traced another line streaking down the window. It was as close as he could come to wiping the tears seeping from his heart.

"We all of us make mistakes, lad. Our only hope for a genuine turning comes when we take a good hard look at our direction. We do that, we're bound to see ourselves as the real problem. So what to do? I, for one, only found a lasting solution in turning to God. Has this halted the blunders I make? Look around, lad. See for yourself. Our need for a Savior remains with us for always. Through Him we find the strength for honest reflection, confession, repentance, prayer, healing, and change." He offered Taylor his spread fingers. "Do feel free to point out whichever of these you've managed on your own."

Taylor did not remove his hand from the window.

"It's not enough to merely act, lad. You've moved and you've acted all your life. Real change, *eternal* change, is when your actions are meant to draw you closer to your Lord." Jonah dropped his arms to his side. "The first act of genuine turning is recognizing that what you have done on your own,

135

what you are *capable* of doing, is not enough. The second act is acknowledging who you are turning *toward*."

FOUR TIMES EACH DAY, THE IONA COMMUNITY'S WORK halted. Most of those present gathered in the central abbey. There was no requirement. Nothing was dictated to anyone. But when the lone bell tolled for the afternoon prayers, a procession began from every point on the compass.

That afternoon Taylor stood outside the church's rear entrance, sheltered from the wind and the rain by an overhang that extended to join with an exterior passageway. People who passed him smiled silent greetings and picked up prayer books from the chair by the door. His chest cavity felt open to both the elements and the inspection of all who passed. Taylor considered himself a private person. Yet he found himself so bound to these folk he could stand exposed and aching before them.

Brother Jonah was one of the last to arrive. If he found anything remarkable in how Taylor stood waiting for him, the brother did not show it. Instead he simply picked up two prayer missals and placed one in Taylor's hands, then held the door for them both.

The abbey was remarkable for maintaining the medieval spirit, both inside and out. Even the stained-glass windows held to a somewhat primitive air. The benches were thick Scottish oak, the floor slate, the air already filled with collective prayers when they took their seats. Brother Jonah found the page in Taylor's book, then let him be.

A plainsong was followed by an Old Testament reading, then another hymn, then the New Testament reading, a third song, then the Gospel passage. Some people seated themselves. Taylor followed Brother Jonah's example, unhooked a padded square from the seat back in front of him, and knelt. But the first line of the communal prayer stopped him. *Lord, lead me from the darkness of my own making.*

The others proceeded down the page. Taylor remained caught by the first line, feeling it resonate through him. His entire being hummed slightly from the impact. A darkness of his own making. Oh yes. These words were a terrible gift, one that had been waiting centuries for him to arrive.

AFTER PRAYERS THEY RETURNED TO THE KITCHEN together. The evening meal was prepared in silence. Taylor had nothing to say. Brother Jonah refrained from his customary quarrels with the kitchen and the meal. As time wore on, it seemed to Taylor that the air took on a new thickness. Far more than the steam and the cooking fragrances congealed around him. Even his breathing took on a new significance.

The change was noticeable to others. The servers who entered seemed instantly aware of something at work. They did not speak a word to either of the cooks. They accepted the food and the utensils and departed casting strange looks at the pair of them. Jonah, for his part, continued to move about in an alien state, not even looking Taylor's way. Several times, however, when Taylor glanced over he thought he saw the brother's lips moving.

When the food was all inside and the others seated, Taylor wiped down the counter, set the towel aside, and followed Jonah into the dining hall. As they passed through the door, he asked quietly, "Have you been praying?"

"Hard as I know how, lad."

The burning began then, so strong it felt as if the backs of his eyes were melting. "For me?"

Jonah pointed him into a chair. "For us all."

EVENING PRAYERS WERE AN HOUR AFTER DINNER. TAYLOR tried to follow the routine, but too many words impacted him. They buffeted his brain like verbal fists. They rose off the page. They shouted at him. He wanted to rage, to weep, to flee. He did nothing. The others sat and stood and sang and chanted and prayed. Taylor endured an isolation as harsh as any he had ever known. Now, this time, he realized he had only himself to blame.

He did not say anything to Jonah after the prayers. What was there to say? He simply returned to his bunk, undressed, and escaped into sleep.

Sometime in the night, a hand reached through his slumber and shook him awake. Taylor wanted to shrug off the hand and roll over and pretend the invitation had not been made. Instead, he dressed and washed his face and followed Jonah back to the abbey. He did not know why. Only that he had no choice.

A midnight prayer vigil was gathering. Most of the brothers were in attendance, as well as a handful of visitors like himself. The air was scented by incense burning at the altar and vigil candles and the nighttime chill.

The New Testament reading came from the thirteenth chapter of 1 Corinthians. Once more, Taylor found himself unable to move past a single passage. One of only three words, yet they captured him and froze him to that point in time. *Love never fails.*

He read the passage over and over and over. How was it possible to write such a thing? His entire life was testimony to the lie of those words. Love failed constantly! There was nothing *less* permanent than love.

The words resonated through him like silent detonations. He felt his interior shatter like glass. The shards fell in silent rain to the floor around him, detritus from this internal war. Taylor looked around him, but no one else seemed to have noticed his destruction.

He raised the book and reread the passage, hoping against hope that he would be able to scoff and turn the tide back and resume the life he felt was now lost and gone forever.

Love never fails.

He erupted from his seat and sprang through the rear door. He raced away from the buildings. The words echoed like a butcher's mirth, chasing him away.

He felt his heart raging against his own mind, tearing himself in two. What was he doing here? Why had he come? To resurrect a love he had himself reduced to ashes? Who was he kidding? The island's stillness chased him on. He did not *belong* here. This was *madness*.

Taylor ran with arms outstretched, desperately seeking to flee the bitter night.

TAYLOR RETURNED DRENCHED FROM WRESTLING with the storm. He toweled off and collapsed in his bunk. Three times he awoke to the dark. Each time he listened for the signal of internal battle rejoined. Yet he sensed nothing save bone-deep weariness. He decided this must be the true flavor of defeat. His dreams were empty descents into blackness.

He awoke early and lay in his bed as his bunkmates went through their morning motions. He was finally roused by the chapel bell.

The sky was still a dismal gray. The stone chapel was unchanged. The interior remained too cold and dim. Taylor took the seat next to Brother Jonah, whose only greeting was to find the place in the prayer missal.

He managed to follow the entire service for the first time. His voice joined with half a hundred others, a monotone of supplicants. Just a bunch of strangers, trying to stay warm by stretching their sleeves over their hands, speaking words from tattered books in ragged unison. Few of them could carry a decent tune. The plainsongs were drowsy monotones, words they could not quite sing together.

Yet as he rose from kneeling over the final prayer, Taylor knew that change was in the air. He still had no idea why he was there. He could say only one thing with any certainty: His own answers were no longer enough.

Love never fails. The constancy of these words marched through his mind with a relentless tread. They formed the backdrop to what he had tried to flee from the night before. It was the same truth he had sought to escape for the past two years. He could avoid this no longer. It was not love that had failed him. He was the one who had failed at love.

Taylor set his prayer book in the pile and followed the others outside, just another penitent rubbing the sleep from his eyes. The empty night had left him no choice. He had been forced to speak the truth that morning. He needed more than he could offer himself.

As they trod the rocky path to the dining hall, sunlight split the heavens and blasted them with silent force. He walked with the others, sniffing the air and blinking confusedly in the light. The brilliance was too alien. He could not quite focus on what he saw.

The woman walking next to him laughed at nothing. Taylor tried but could not quite fashion a smile in reply.

"Do you not see it, then?"

"Sorry, what?"

"Angels are gathered about heaven's altar, singing to the day now born."

He stopped and turned his face upward. The wind was utterly still, the day warming swiftly.

"It's a lovely tune they're singing, is it not?"

"It's lost to me," he softly replied.

"Ah, well. Never you mind. At least you've taken time to have a listen." She almost skipped away. "There will be other days."

"Are you sure?" he asked. But the woman was already gone.

He entered the kitchen and helped Brother Jonah prepare the coffee and slice the bread. For once the man's silent presence was welcome. Taylor waited until the chores were finished to say, "I need to leave the island for a while."

Jonah replied to the sunlight splashed upon the kitchen window. "The others will be bereft to hear it."

"Others?"

"The ones forced to take your place in here with me."

Jonah stood by the sink, so intent upon his mug and the radiant view Taylor could examine him minutely. This was clearly an intelligent man. Jonah, too, fought against a nature as contrary and rebellious as Taylor's own. Jonah raged; he rebelled. He lived in constant impatience with a world that did not move as he would have preferred. Jonah reached Taylor because he came from the same realm. Taylor listened because he identified with the man and his internal strife. Even Jonah's silence contained questions sharp as lances. They probed deep. What could possibly cause this man to pray for a stranger he had every reason to distrust? What did Jonah possess that made him able to speak with such confidence about matters Taylor had never uttered even to himself?

Taylor wrestled with a desire to say what he could not put into words. He made do with a hand on the brother's shoulder. Jonah sipped from his mug and asked the window, "I'll be seeing you again?"

Taylor turned for the door. "Count on it."

BY THE TIME TAYLOR ARRIVED AT THE ISLAND'S PORT, THE day had warmed enough that he found his sweater uncomfortable. Clouds had been banished with the wind. He paid his fare, stepped onto the boat, and joined the others by the railing. The change was so great Taylor found it hard to even recall the gray Scotland that had greeted him on his arrival.

And there were waves. Great rollers untouched by wind lifted the boat and propelled it in swooping dives down to the next swell.

Taylor carried the monastery with him. The previous night's internal bruising was as raw a presence as the building sense of pressure. He was being propelled forward. Toward what, he could not say. But there was a sense of motion at every level of his being.

Taylor watched the jewellike sea's rise and fall and accepted for the first time that there was no avoiding his own lack. Not anymore. He felt surrounded by everything his own life did not contain.

If he was ever to understand what all this meant, he needed help beyond himself. He needed a wisdom he did not possess, and never would so long as he insisted upon seeking alone.

Taylor arrived at the mainland harbor and headed up a lane transformed by daylight. The little village sparkled. Gone was the former seedy barrenness. Even the cobblestones possessed a highland sheen.

He climbed the lane to the surf shop, taking clear aim at the goal ahead. His honesty burned too brightly this day to do otherwise. He hungered for an understanding that would *last*. He wanted that which would not be torn from him the next time he was assaulted by a want, a need, a worry, a pain, an anger, a foe. He wanted to maintain this hunger, to reach forward and grasp and seek and *learn*. He could not do this on his own. He had to receive whatever it was that gave these people the ability to fathom what he could neither see nor even name.

THE RED-BEARDED SCOT WAS ALONE BEHIND THE SURF-shop's counter. He greeted Taylor with a huge grin and the words, "Thought I might find you slinking back today, Flawda."

"Where's your mate?"

"We rolled the dice, and I got stuck with the work detail." He pretended it mattered little. "Never you mind. I'll get me a double portion next go-round."

"Maybe you can get out tomorrow."

"Shows how much you know. Take it when you can; that's the first and only rule of surfing Scots-style." Eyes tightened in merry avarice. "You aiming on giving it a go?"

"No board, no wet suit, no ride to the break."

"Buy the board; we'll loan you the suit and find you the ride."

"Done."

"A couple of blokes showed up last night, fresh caught like yourself. I put them up with a mate of mine, runs a B&B down the lane."

"And took a cut for the service, I bet."

The bearded giant showed a fistful of gleaming teeth. "Stick around these parts long enough, you'll find there's little in life that makes a Scots happier than the next honest quid."

THEY WOULD NEVER HAVE FOUND THE BREAK WITHOUT instructions. Never in a million years.

They followed tiny roads lined with ancient stone walls and hedgerows. They toured the Scottish moors and passed through timeless stone hamlets. All the world was either an emerald green so brilliant it hurt the eye or blue or gray. The same rock that jutted from the earth had been taken and carved and formed by man. Every wall was of this stone, every house, even the roofs with their blankets of lichen. The strongest sounds were of sheep and of perfumed wind blowing through the van's open windows. The roads tracked politely across the fells and around the forests, so in tune with nature the lanes refused to maintain a straight line. Turnings were marked either by ancient stone markers or tiny white signs, both of which were easily missed. The one time they lost their way and asked directions from a passing shepherd, they might as well have begged help from his sheepdog, for all the good it did them. Not even the Brit who drove their creaking van could understand a highland word.

Taylor and his traveling companions had nothing in common save their love of the sea. This and the brilliant day were enough to make for a very pleasant drive. The distance from the surf shop to the break could not have been more than twenty-five miles. It took them over two hours. The only way they knew they had arrived was from the motley collection of cars parked on the wayside. Board straps dangled like beacons from roof racks. They parked tight against a moss-covered wall and pulled out their gear. They set their boards and wet suits across the wall, clambered over, and hiked across the meadow. The ground was hard, the grass stunted. Heather bloomed up a neighboring hillside, the color aching in its purity. Songbirds sprang from half-hidden nests at their approach, chirping frantically to draw their attention away from little ones. In the distance a sheepdog barked. There was not a breath of wind.

The ocean was a muted rush of sound that grew with every step. They mounted a steep rise, crested the ridge, and found themselves staring down at a rocky beach shaped like a sliver of new moon. Ancient fortress walls adorned the high points, with a series of rusted cannon pointed seaward. To their left a watchtower had crumbled into a pile of scenic rubble.

The local surfers had gathered driftwood and started a massive fire near the point. It was a curious way to begin a summer surf on a day in the low eighties. But by the time they made it down the rise and approached the locals, the sea radiated a bitter chill. The waves sounded like the growl of a winter behemoth, one unused to being caged by summer, not even for a single day.

Taylor held back and let his two fellow travelers make the greetings. The locals were neither hostile nor wary. Surfing in water only a few degrees above freezing created a special clanship. A single slip, a bad fall, an unseen rock caught after a wipeout, and suddenly the only thing between the surfer and hypothermia was a watchful mate. When his companions let it slip that Taylor was visiting the Iona cloister, it was good for a bit of gentle ribbing, the sign that even the silent one was welcome this day.

It was not out of shyness that Taylor kept himself aside. He was finding it difficult to come to grips with the sudden canting to his world. He sat on a rocky outcrop at the base of a cliff, well away from the others. They donned suits and hefted boards and called an impatient demand. He waved to their invitation and remained where he was. There was a rightness to the moment. One he could not have discovered until now, seated alone upon this hardscrabble beach. He had been headed here all along. Here to this nameless cove on the coast of an alien land.

He was no longer filled with the tragic isolation that had been his constant burden for so very long. Taylor watched waves rise and roar in a frigid sea and marveled at how easy it seemed. Here in this moment, there was no longer an internal struggle. Nor a sense of shame over his decision.

He bowed his head and said his few words. In truth, it felt as though the words were spoken before they had been formed. The act was that natural. The moment that full.

He lifted his face back to the sun and waited. Perhaps there was a hint of change within his being. All he could say was that he seemed very aware. He noted the rise and fall of his chest. He watched the sunlight being captured by each arriving wave. He heard the crackle of the surfers' fire. He tasted the fragrances of Scotland's summer on his tongue. And somehow found the day incomplete because he could not yet name the seed planted at the very core of his being.

THE WET SUIT LOANED TO HIM BY THE SURF SHOP WAS the thickest rubber he had ever worn, five millimeters on the chest, three in the legs and arms, titanium ribbing throughout. Boots cinched beneath the suit. He squatted in the shore waves and waxed his new board thoroughly, the water's chill burning into his exposed face and hands. He rose and stepped into the water. The cold bit like acid. He squinted into the afternoon sun, waiting for another of the regular lulls. Then he gripped his board and dove under, screaming into the next incoming wave to punch away the cold.

It took most of the paddle and three more dousings before the cold stopped burning so bad he could only bear it by shouting. The locals continued their good-natured jesting of the visiting pansies. Taylor sat slightly away from them, knowing he was welcome to move to the point but still preferring his own company. He caught his first wave because the others shouted at him to move.

His first ride was not a particularly large wave, but the form was perfect. It peeled with the constancy of a liquid orchestra. He scarcely needed to move. He stood with arms outstretched, gliding like a black highland gull upon neoprene wings.

He paddled back out and sat drinking great draughts of the hyperchilled air. The cold no longer bit so much as embraced. He could not capture enough of this day. He continued to sweep around, making circles upon his board, studying the cliffs and the ruins and the waves and the sky. The locals watched him good-naturedly, clearly approving of this silent stranger whose eyes were frozen in a wide-open state, gorging upon the beauty of their homeland.

The next set was huge, lumbering beasts of crystal and blue. Taylor waited his turn, then rode and swooped and shouted with glee.

Upon his return, he recognized a difference. In truth, it was just another day. Another ocean, another group communing upon another coast. The same, yet different. Yet the change was not outside. Nor was it something shouted. Taylor made another slow circle upon his board and finally pierced the subtle puzzle. He was not grieving. He was not accompanied by all the mistakes of his forlorn past. They were not gone; no, that would have been asking too much. But they did not *own* him. This moment, this day, he was made anew. He caught another wave, and another after that one. And he felt in truth that he had found his own chapel, a place where he could sit upon a pew of fiberglass and ocean and listen to the day's celestial song.

THE BRIT'S NAME WAS KENNY DEAN; THE CALIFORNIA
guy riding shotgun was Red Harris. They traded tales on the
way back, or at least the pair in the front seat did while Taylor
mostly listened. They did not pry overmuch.

Surfers were perhaps the most eclectic bunch on the planet.
Kenny was a wanderer by trade. He spoke of breaks around
the globe with intense fondness. The two Americans knew not
to ask about his job. Wanderers usually hated work and did it
out of necessity. Red was spending a summer living his dream

between university and the real world. Red had hooked up with Kenny when looking for someone to share traveling expenses. Normal landlocked topics of conversation were passed over as inconsequential. The talk revolved around where they had surfed last, where they were going next, where to stay, what to eat, when the waves were due to arrive.

Kenny's van was in abysmal shape. The bolts holding Taylor's rear seat in place had rusted through. He was kept from flying over backward by a surf leash attached in triangular fashion to the front seat and one door handle. The motor was louder than the stereo, which possessed four blown speakers and a cassette deck that ate tapes. The van's rear was blanketed by swaths of black smoke. The interior smelled of overripe wet suits and a rain-washed tent and rank sleeping bags and damp towels and surf wax. A crate rattled at Taylor's feet, containing dirty crockery and cans of tonight's dinner. The four tires were utterly bald.

All this made for a glorious ride.

When Taylor did not offer his own turn at how he came to be where he was, talk moved to where the pair in the front seats were headed next. They were basically open to anywhere. The problem was funds. They had been sleeping in a tent until the recent rains flooded the campsite. The previous two nights in a B&B had pretty much emptied the larder. Red was two weeks away from returning to California and his own personal nine-to-five dungeon. His wallet was almost as bare as Kenny's.

Clouds were gathering by the time they arrived back in the

Scottish harbor town. A gentle sea breeze was wafting in with the sunset. But the western horizon was thick and black, dimming the day's final light to seamless gray. The little village was once again a place of grim and colorless stone. Only a few swatches of gold and copper overhead reflected the glory they had found at Castle Bay. They halted at the port and the pair helped Taylor unload his gear. They did not even pretend to object when Taylor paid handsomely for the day's outing.

In the midst of their farewells, Taylor spotted Brother Jonah seated upon a quayside bench. "Can you guys hang on here for just a second?"

"No problems." Kenny possessed the perpetual patience and good cheer of a seasoned traveler. "With what you've just handed over, we've got ourselves enough for a bed and a bath and a pint along with our beans."

Brother Jonah was on his feet by the time Taylor arrived. He wore thick wool socks beneath open-toed sandals, shapeless denim trousers, a tattered knit pullover, and a very grim expression. "We've had visitors while you were away."

"They were looking for Kirra?"

"They were asking questions. Improper questions. Questions you saw fit to keep to yourself."

Taylor realized the bag at Jonah's feet was his own. "You're kicking me out?"

"No, lad. But I am wondering if perhaps it is time for you to go."

"I'm not ready."

"Which is as good a sign as any that your coming here was ordained by God." Jonah guided them both down onto the stone bench. "They were also asking about you."

"I don't know who they are."

"If you did, I wouldn't care to hear."

Taylor's limbs felt thick and cottony from the surf. His bones still ached slightly from the water's bite. His mind felt sluggish and resentful of being dragged back into the here and now. "What do you want me to do?"

To his astonishment, Jonah beamed in approval. "Ah, lad, that is a fine question indeed. You come, you bare your soul, you trust an old man enough to worship with him, and now you speak as an acolyte to his teacher."

"That's how I feel."

"The Good Book tells us we must hold only one Teacher at the forefront. We must seek endlessly to know His will for us. Do you fathom what I'm telling you?"

"I think so."

"The stripping away you've started here is a lifelong quest. We all grow at God's timing, and where God plants us."

"You *are* sending me away."

Jonah's tone was as kindly as Taylor had ever heard it. "You came with one quest; you found yourself another. That doesn't mean the first has lost its importance. Life's responsibilities don't end with the finding of God. We must seek Him through all things. We seek in service as well as through prayer. We allow the story of our lives to be rewritten by His hand." He patted Taylor's knee. "Never you mind, lad. You'll understand this in the proper time."

"But I don't know where to go."

"Aye, and that brings us to the task at hand." He turned and stared out to sea. "When I'm not occupied in the kitchen, I run the Iona library and help with the collation of documents. You have heard of our work?"

"You're gathering information on herbs and medieval remedies."

"Believers like to assume that the Age of Enlightenment and scientific reasoning caused the schism between faith and medicine. We now know that the rift goes much further back. We've discovered fragments of forgotten texts. We're detailing medical treatments back through the Dark Ages. We've learned that physicians thought it impossible to be well in body but ill in spirit. Everywhere and always, God was referred to as their partner in healing.

"But at this same point in time, the Church was losing sway. Nations were being born, wars fought. The last thing the Church needed was another threat from within. What would happen to priests' authority if patients listened to their physicians first? So around the year 1200, the Church issued an edict. All physicians were ordered to stop referring to God in their work. Medical texts that included God in the healing process were heaped in city squares and put to the torch. Doctors who invoked God's name were branded as heretics.

"But some healers held to the old ways. If discovered, mind, they'd be burned at the stake. So they concealed themselves, their ways, their patients. They continued to seek a marriage between God and healing. They argued that God's creation held numerous secrets, including the mysteries of good health. Such secrets could only be discovered with God's help. For their troubles, these healers were hunted and branded and lashed and murdered."

A sudden blast of wind shunted through the harbor, blowing whitecaps across the waters and sending the gray wall scuttling closer. Taylor huddled deeper in his anorak and said, "You found some records that have survived."

"Remnants mostly. But yes, some have surfaced, and these have led us to others. Kirra was seeking to track down one such relic." Brother Jonah slipped his hand into his pocket and passed over a folded slip of paper. "One of our sources is a healer working in the Basque country in the borderlands between France and Spain. You have heard of this region?"

Taylor nodded.

"Excellent. I suggest you travel there."

"Thank you."

Jonah drew Taylor to his feet. "You will take the advice of a grouchy old man?"

"Always."

"When you find yourself faced with impossible choices,

remember this. God's path is called the narrow way. Not because it is more difficult, but because it is *restricted*."

"Restricted how?"

Jonah offered Taylor his hand. "I would say that makes an excellent question to carry along with you."

THE PAIR STOOD BY THEIR VAN AND PRETENDED NOT TO have been watching. "All right there?"

"Fine." Taylor dropped his bag by his board. "I'm sort of in a jam."

Kenny did not seem surprised. "Seeing as how you're not overloose with the words, I sort of figured you for carting around some worries and woe."

"I need a ride south."

"How far south?"

"Across the English Channel."

"Ah. Running from the law, are we?"

Taylor waved that off. "I'll pay."

"Whereabouts in France are you headed?"

"Let's leave that for the time being, okay?"

"France," Kenny mused. "Haven't been there in years, strangely enough."

"Heard they've got some killer surf," Red offered.

"Aye, that they do. You'll pay; did I hear you rightly?"

"All expenses for all of us."

Kenny offered his brilliant grin. "I like the sound of that, mate. You're on."

THEY DROPPED TAYLOR AT THE SURF SHOP AND WENT BACK to the guesthouse to pack the rest of their gear. The red-bearded Scot greeted him with, "Hear you've not done too bad for yourself, Flawda."

"The name is Taylor. Can I use your phone? I need to call America. I'll pay you back."

"Aye, I suppose we can work something out." He cut down the music and tossed Taylor a cordless phone. "Make your call."

He moved to the back of the shop. Since it was Saturday, he dialed Allison's home number. She answered with a very sleepy hello.

"I'm really sorry to wake you. What time is it?"

"You obviously don't have kids."

"Excuse me?"

"Saturday I play catch-up on my rest. When she's sleeping, I'm sleeping." There was the rustle of bedcovers. "Where are you?"

"Scotland."

"Where?"

"I really shouldn't say anything more than that."

Allison returned to her customary chill. "You still don't trust me."

"I want to."

"Do you?"

"Yes."

"I suppose that will have to do for now. Is everything okay?"

"Things," he replied softly, "aren't so good."

"What's the matter?"

He debated a long moment, then decided one issue needed to be out and in the open. "I'm over here looking for Kirra Revell."

"As in Revell Pharmaceuticals?"

"Yes. She's gone missing." He took a breath. "She and I were, well . . ."

"I've got the picture, Taylor."

"It was years ago. But I never got over it."

"I figured you carried a torch for someone." A long breath, then, "Let me know if you find yourself ready to move on."

He tasted several responses. But none of them fit the moment.

She accepted his silence with a brisk lack of surprise. "I've done some checking, like you asked."

"Be careful, Allison."

"I don't think it will go any further than our tame lab rats. Besides, these are pretty open secrets, what I found. Revell's been going through a rough patch. Four new products failed in the last year and a half, one at the stage-three level."

His mind slipped into the old work grooves with discomforting ease. New product development went through fixed stages. Once a new drug had been identified and tested on animals, testing on humans began. Stage-three trials were the toughest and most expensive, usually conducted at a university teaching hospital. To lose a product at the stage-three level meant that although the product was successful at treating an illness, its side effects proved so severe the FDA refused to authorize it for general release. By this point, research and development costs on a new drug could exceed two hundred million dollars. To lose four new products in eighteen months, and one at stage three, was catastrophic even for a company as large as Revell.

But it did not explain why Amanda was tying Taylor's finding of Kirra to the acquisition of his company. Unless it was an empty threat. Which did not sound like Amanda to him. Not at all.

Allison continued, "As a result, Amanda went through the Revell Corporation with a wrecking ball. The two senior product-development directors have been axed. Same goes for the heads of two labs. Everybody else is working double overtime and sweating bullets. They are being pushed to bring in results in no time flat. The lawyers are fighting their way through the courts to maintain patents on three products scheduled for generic competition. And ours is not the only acquisition they're working on."

The two travelers chose that moment to reenter the shop. Taylor turned his back on the chatter. "What?"

"They've made another acquisition. Finalized just three weeks ago. A company called Geneco Labs."

"The name rings a very vague bell."

"I checked them out, but my papers are back in the office."

"Tell me what you remember."

"Started about six years ago by an anesthesiologist and a

nervous system bioclinician. Three products on market, all specialty anesthesia and surgery related. What was interesting was the purchase price. Eight hundred million dollars, a straight cash buyout. Triple the company's current market valuation."

Behind him the three men laughed uproariously. Taylor turned far enough to see they were bent over a map spread upon the counter. He hunched further over the phone. "I think this might be what we're looking for."

"What does it mean?"

"Geneco Labs must have a silver bullet. A product they're almost ready to bring to market." It couldn't be anything else. Taylor was thinking out loud now, fighting off the noise behind him, keeping his mind focused. "The company has been keeping it quiet in order to maximize the lead time between its release and another company developing a competing product."

"But we're in eye products," Allison complained. "Why would Revell threaten us with dropping the acquisition?"

"I have no idea. Unless they're just running out of cash and they're looking for an excuse."

The men started laughing again. The Scot called over, "Time's up, Flawda! You're talking out the tide!"

Allison asked, "Where are you?"

"A surf shop." He deflected further questions with, "I don't want you to get into danger."

"But you need to know what that new Geneco Labs product is."

"Not if you're going to be at risk."

"It's okay, Taylor. I have my sources too, you know."

"Just be careful."

"Are you coming home soon?"

"That I can't say yet."

"Things aren't the same without you in the next office."

Once more he caught the tone and all that was unsaid. Only this time he felt his heart touched and did not mind. Over the phone he heard a child's singing. "Is that your daughter?"

"Yes, my little angel has just woken up." In an instant, Allison switched from business colleague to warm-hearted mother. "Clarissa's going to be four next month, aren't you, sweetie? She's growing up on me."

"I bet you're a terrific mom."

"I try. I try very, very hard."

"Yank!"

"I have to go, Allison."

"You take care as well. Gowers is still down most days, asking questions I can't answer."

"I'll call you Monday." Taylor punched off the phone, turned around, and said, "Let's move."

Taylor fought good-naturedly with Red over who would occupy the wobbly rear seat. He pretended to become involved in their excitement over having both money and a new destination. But his last view of the Scottish coastland was of a somber cloud wall pushing hard for land.

THE SIX-HUNDRED-MILE JOURNEY FROM OBAN
to Portsmouth took two very long days. The van proved
reliable but slow and possessed as strong a personality as any
of them. Hammering the gas pedal meant nothing. The van
chose its own pace and maintained it no matter what they
did or shouted. Kenny and Red treated Taylor's secrecy as
prime entertainment. They spent hours musing over what
dire deed Taylor had committed. By the time they finally
arrived at the cross-channel ferry, Kenny was certain they

carted a bank robber, while Red held to suspicions of serious embezzlement.

The Portsmouth-Cherbourg ferry was eleven stories tall and held three hundred cars. Taylor tried to call Amanda from a phone booth in the ship's lobby. When an impersonal voice told him to leave a message, he hung up and punched in Allison's number. It was seven o'clock in the evening, Maryland time, when she answered. Taylor could hear a child crying in the background. "Allison?"

"Oh, Taylor. Are you all right?"

"Fine. What's the matter with your daughter?"

"The doctor says it's just a cold." Allison closed a door, which did not entirely shut out the noise. "Clarissa has a fever. She hates being sick. She gets angry with the entire world. Just like her mother."

"You sound tired. Exhausted."

"There are days when it's hard keeping all the balls in the air. This is one of them."

"I can call back."

"No. No. To be honest, it's nice having an adult to talk to right now. But I don't have anything for you. I've had to take time off to be with her, and my tame techie is on vacation until the day after tomorrow."

"Did you get the money I sent?"

"I wish you hadn't done this, Taylor."

"Why?"

"What am I going to do with ten thousand dollars?"

"You told me yourself you could use it."

"I haven't had spare cash lying around since the divorce. Now I've got your ten plus the other two stuffed in a grocery bag in the basement."

He knew he needed to determine whether she could be trusted. But the motive stank of subterfuge. Taylor remained too caught up in the honesty of Iona for half-lies. So he asked what was front and center in his mind. "What happened to your marriage, Allison? You're beautiful; you've got a super mind. You're funny, affectionate. You're clearly a great mother."

"The whole package, right?"

"I'm sorry. I shouldn't pry."

"I don't have anybody but myself to blame. Everybody told me I was making a terrible mistake. But I knew better. I did what I wanted. Isn't that what beautiful girls are supposed to be able to do?"

The phone booth was lined on three sides with red velour. The other was a glass wall opening to the main deck. He cupped the mouthpiece to cover the bedlam of holiday-makers traipsing by.

Allison went on, "I lied to myself as long as I could. But one day I woke up alone. Again. I knew my ex was out catting around town. Again. I couldn't let my baby girl grow up with such an example to follow. I know I did the right thing. No. I did the *only* thing." There was a catch to her voice now, a struggle that turned every word into half a sob. "Some days, though, I feel like such a fool."

He uncovered the bottom half of the phone. "No, Allison. You were absolutely right. And wise."

"Where are you?"

"On a ferry."

Her mind remained locked upon what his question had uncovered. "It's such a hard thing, looking in the mirror and wondering how I could have felt so right about anything and ended up being so wrong."

"You didn't make the mistake, Allison. He did."

"I wish that were only—"

"Listen to me." His voice was loud enough to attract the attention of a tourist waiting for the phone. Taylor turned away. "What did you do? You loved a man so much you wanted to give him your life. You wanted to make a family. You gave him a daughter. You *loved* him, Allison. He was just too much a self-absorbed jerk to recognize what he had. The guy should be taken out and shot."

"At least we agree on that much." She paused, then asked a question of her own. "What happened to you?"

Taylor opened his mouth, but no sound emerged. What could he say? That he was the same kind of fool as her ex? That he deserved no better fate than to go through life alone? That he had shattered the heart of a good woman? That Kirra had just managed to suss him out in time?

Allison went on, "You're carrying a torch for somebody; you said that yourself. Did she burn you?"

He shook his head, defeated by his inability to lie anymore. "I wish."

"What?"

"I was too big a fool to realize what I had until it was gone."

"Well, then." Allison's voice lowered to a throaty burr. "Maybe you better make sure it never happens to you again."

THE TRIP FROM THE FERRY PORT OF CHERBOURG TO Biarritz was a 550-mile trek straight south. Late on the first day, they finally left the last of the chill North Sea gray behind. Their entire second day was a journey through increasingly brilliant illumination. Rolling emerald hills basked beneath a cloudless summer sky. The air was scented with a thousand flavors, all of them French.

At Biarritz they pulled off the autoroute, halted at a petrol station, and were greeted by rolling clouds of sea mist. Thunder echoed in a blue Basque sky.

The address Brother Jonah had slipped into Taylor's pocket was for a Jacques Dupin, whose address was a farm outside Guethary. Taylor expected serious dissent from his companions when he insisted they first go there before checking the surf. But Kenny merely shrugged and said, "Our journey's been paved by your open wallet, mate. Let's do the thing fast; that's all I ask."

The village of Guethary was framed by rolling green hills and carefully tended farms. One-lane country roads wound tight ribbons around herds of cattle, late-summer crops, bleating sheep, and whitewashed Basque farms. The three of them became so hopelessly lost it took two hours just to find their way back to the highway and the same petrol station.

Beneath a steadily descending sun, Taylor went inside and begged for help. The Frenchman behind the counter did not understand English, but his eyebrows rose at the name on Brother Jonah's slip of paper. He nodded vigorously, pulled out his cell phone, squinted over Jonah's writing, and dialed.

He spoke at length, then handed Taylor the phone. A woman's voice chirped something. Taylor replied, "Do you speak English?"

"Yes, a little. Who is this, please?"

"I'm looking for Mr. Dupin."

"All the world looks for my Jacques. Who is speaking?"

"My name is Taylor Knox."

"I am not knowing this name."

"Brother Jonah sent me."

"Ah! From the holy island, yes? The man in the, how you say, *bibliothèque?*"

"Library."

"Of course, the library. How is the good brother?"

"Grouchy."

When she laughed, she sounded no more than fifteen. "I see we speak of the same man. You wish to come?"

"I tried, but we got lost."

"Yes, yes, is impossible to find until you know the way. Like so much of life, yes? Please, you give me back the other man. I will explain."

The station attendant accepted the phone, nodded vigorously, then hung up and drew Taylor a detailed map.

By the time Taylor left the station, the shadows were as long as the faces of his two companions. "I'm really sorry about all this."

"Aye, well, we're all worn out from the travels." Kenny tried to make light of his disappointment. "No telling what would've happened if we went straight from the road to twenty-foot surf."

"I guess we could get wet and do this after."

"Too late for that now." Kenny opened the driver's door. "You know where we're headed this time?"

Even with the map it took them until almost dark. The Dupin home was just another Basque farmhouse, white with clay-tiled roof and red shutters. The lane was shaded by a tunnel of ancient trees that changed the day's final light into ethereal gloaming. An old woman the size of a child opened the door as they chugged to a halt. "Are you a friend of God's island?"

Taylor stepped forward. "Mrs. Dupin?"

"Come inside, all of you."

"You go ahead, mate." Neither Kenny nor Red showed any

interest in leaving the van. "We'll just sit here and enjoy being still for a change."

Mrs. Dupin did not insist. She held the door open for Taylor, then led him into a brightly lit kitchen. Herbs hung in tight bunches from every conceivable nook. Wildflowers dried in sheaves above both windows. The three central beams were so decked out as to be almost lost behind their loads. "You will have an *infusion,* yes?"

"I don't want to be a bother, ma'am."

"What is bother? Sit, sit, you are too big for me when you stand." She was an ancient crone, dark and wizened and strong as petrified wood. With eyes of black light, she watched him take in the chamber. "You are liking my kitchen?"

"Very much. It smells like a meadow."

"My husband, he gathers these." She pulled down a clay jar from a shelf and extracted a handful of herbs which she tossed into a teapot. She took a bubbling pot from the stove and poured in water. "All the time he is walking and picking plants and talking with God."

Taylor accepted the news with his cup. "He isn't here?"

"He is far up now, very high." She pointed out the window to mountains turned gold by the setting sun. "Searching for his autumn plants in heaven's valleys."

"How long will he be gone?"

"Ah, Monsieur." The woman was scarcely taller than Taylor even when he was seated. She laughed like a young maiden, shyly hiding her smile behind her hand. "What woman knows how long her man is gone when he leaves?"

"Do you know Kirra Revell?"

"So many people come to speak with my Jacques. So many names."

"A tall American, blond, late twenties. Very beautiful. She too was sent by Brother Jonah."

"I pay so little attention to my husband's patients. More tea?"

Taylor accepted the polite turndown because he had no choice. He drank his tea and thanked her and departed. Night was gathering, a peaceful descent into pastoral rest. Crows cackled in the neighboring trees. Cowbells tinkled in time to his footsteps across the gravel. Somewhere in the distance a child laughed. Kenny called across the dark, "Found what you're after, then?"

"Almost." He slid into the backseat. "I'm sorry about holding you guys up."

"Like I said, mate. We're just dancing to the piper's tune."

"Yeah, well, the least I can do is buy you both a bed, a bath, and a great French meal."

The van started with a sputter and a roar. Kenny turned to flash him a grand smile. "Sounds like a proper bribe to me."

Taylor watched the farmhouse disappear behind the first line of trees, then turned back to his companions. After driving four days and arriving to the sound of huge surf, it was great how well the pair were handling their frustration.

Or so he thought at the time.

TAYLOR SWAM IN A BLACKNESS SO THICK HE DID
not even need to breathe. Or so it seemed, until the hands
gripped his neoprene suit and lifted his face into the sunlight.

Then it came back to him in a rush. The drive down the
lengths of both England and France. The arrival in Guethary.
The surf. The shooter.

The instant he came fully awake, the burning in his chest
became so great he convulsed. He sucked and sucked, his lungs

filling with such rapidity he choked and gasped and sprayed all the air out again.

A massive inside wash bore straight down at them. Taylor felt Kenny's arms tighten around his chest. Kenny's grip was as bad as the holddown, so tight Taylor could not take a second breath.

To either side of them came a pair of musical eruptions. Bullets drilled into the water. Even in his semi-aware state, Taylor knew the shooter was still there and hunting. But all he could think of was air. He plucked futilely at Kenny's arms.

The wave smashed them with velvet ease, tearing him effortlessly from Kenny's grip. He struggled and searched for the surface, his movements turned cottony and slow. He broke through and heaved a breath. Taylor coughed and hacked and felt his lungs seared by the salt spume. He breathed again. He could hear the shooter more clearly now. The rifle's boom was a echoing thunder.

The shooter had studied both lair and prey. He knew Taylor had just one way to return to land. One escape route from the bone-crushing inside break. The shooter's position gave him a complete sweep of the rock-strewn beach.

But the shooter had made one grave miscalculation. The inside wash was a constant tumult. The waves rocked and pummeled and pushed. The ocean was covered with a thick layer of froth. Beneath that, the sea was a murky translucence from the silt and seaweed. Which was the only reason Taylor was still alive.

The next wave was far larger. Taylor was sent to the bottom

yet again. A rock appeared out of nowhere and gave his head a glancing blow. This time Taylor almost welcomed the release.

Taylor came to as a hand slapped his face. Kenny leaned over him and shouted, "Get it together, mate. I can't do this alone!"

He managed to draw his feet under him and push through the wash as Kenny carried him up to dry land. As soon as they were clear of the sea, Kenny dropped him like a sack. Which did his chest and his head no good whatsoever. But Kenny was already racing for the cliff path.

Taylor's brain managed one final thought: At least somebody still wanted him alive.

TAYLOR AWOKE FROM A DREAM ABOUT THE IONIAN monastery. He had been seated in the old chapel. The flagstone floors were bowed and worn by eleven centuries of sandals and bare feet. Brother Jonah had been repeating the same words Taylor had carried with him since leaving the holy isle. He opened his eyes to the sound of Jonah talking about eternal choices. And took the dream as a sign of just how close he had come to that final door.

The setting sun painted his room in burnished gold and overlong shadows. The hospital room smelled vaguely of chemicals and the fecal odor of long-ago illnesses. His bed was too firm and too well starched. Sounds slipped under his closed door and rebounded in a room of hard surfaces.

A nurse was noting something into his records. She gave him a professional smile and spoke in French. Taylor smiled back, glad to be hearing something that confirmed he was still firmly bound to the here and now.

She left and came back with a doctor, who gave Taylor a cursory inspection, spending most of his time around Taylor's bandaged head.

Everything ached. Taylor's lungs felt scraped raw from salt water. The holddowns came back to him in vivid flashes: the sunlight streaming through the breaking surf, the silt rushing back and forth beneath the incoming wave, the bullets plunging through the surface. He felt the rough intimacy of hugging that underwater rock as his lungs shrieked for air. He saw the shooter's rifle aimed straight for his head and felt the cold black wind suck at his life's breath once more.

The doctor pointed to the white bandage around Taylor's chest and spoke words in French. Taylor did as the doctor ordered and breathed more deeply than was comfortable. The pain was strong but not stabbing. The rib appeared bruised but not cracked through. The doctor observed his face closely, probed several times, and nodded his satisfaction.

The doctor left. The nurse walked to the doorway and said something in French. Two policemen entered the room. They saluted the bed, which Taylor found mildly amusing. The nurse hurried over, tilted up his bed, then filled a plastic cup with water. She spoke with musical sharpness to the policeman while tapping her watch, then departed.

The senior policeman took the room's one chair while Taylor drained the cup and poured himself another. The junior cop remained by the door. "I am Lieutenant Armand. This is Corporal Saliere. You are American, yes?"

"That's right. Where am I?"

"The Biarritz hospital. Your name?"

"Taylor Knox."

"Spell this, please."

Taylor did so. "Did you catch the shooter?"

"The shooter. Yes. Interesting that someone would try to assassinate a surfer. This is not usual on the Basque coast. Do you know this man?"

"I couldn't see his face. But I don't think so."

"It is normal that you have people shooting rifles at you while you surf?"

"First time ever."

"But you do not seem surprised."

"I was shocked at the time. Now I'm just glad to be alive."

"Alive. Yes. Another surfer saved your life, according to the witnesses on the cliff. You know this man?"

"Kenny Dean." Taylor spelled this as well. "Is he okay?"

"We would like to ask him the same question. Unfortunately Monsieur Dean ran from the scene."

"What?"

"We will come back to that in a moment. You left your belongings with this man? Money, perhaps? Or other valuables?"

"No, I left everything at our hotel."

"You traveled alone with this Monsieur Dean?"

"There was one other surfer with us, Red Harris."

"They are both American?"

"Kenny is British. Red is from California."

"You have known them long?"

"We met surfing in Scotland a few days ago. I hitched a ride south with them."

"You were shot at surfing in Scotland also?"

"No. I told you. This was the first time."

"You must excuse me, Mr. Knox. Do I say that correctly? Knox. Yes. Your reaction surprises me. You were shot at by a man armed with what seems to be an assassin's rifle. You were saved by a man you have known only a few days. He risked his own life chasing a shooter, while he was himself unarmed. You are sure you can offer no explanations?"

"I'm sorry. No."

The lieutenant spent a long moment studying Taylor. "I suggest you try and remember more than you are offering us, Monsieur. The waves were good that day, yes?"

"The best I've ever seen."

"Our foreign surfing guests are most welcome here. But there are rules they must follow on land, just as in the sea. These rules are for their safety, and for the safety of our own people. I fear you have broken these rules. It would help if you cooperated."

"I'm telling you all I know."

"That is still to be determined." The questions followed a calm and persistent course. Did he know of anyone who might want to see him dead? Where had he traveled before Scotland? How did he arrive here? Describe the journey, please. Confirm places you stayed along the way. Give us a contact name at your company in America.

Taylor's entire body pulsed with growing pain by the time the policeman stopped his questioning. He wanted the men to leave, but he needed to know, "Did you speak with my friends?"

"Friends, yes. An interesting word." The senior policeman seemed to have been waiting for that question. "Interesting that one friend would pull you from the surf and race up to attack a man armed with a rifle. Interesting also that when the shooter fled, so did both your friends."

"Have you found them?"

"No, Monsieur Knox, we have found no one and nothing. Not the shooter, not your friends, not a reason for why you are here in a French hospital and lucky to be alive. Monsieur Dean was observed driving away in a Ford Econoline van with British plates. He and another man." The lieutenant had hard dark eyes that noticed everything. "You are surprised by this?"

"The clothes I was wearing before the surf were in that van." But little else. Taylor had left most of his things at the small hotel. But that was not something he particularly wanted to discuss with the cop. Especially not the money.

"We believe Mr. Dean and his associate drove across the Spanish border. We have made a request to our Spanish colleagues for assistance. Are you sure you cannot help us find answers to these very important questions?"

"I've told you everything I know."

"That I doubt very much, Monsieur. You will please give me your passport."

"Sorry, all my things are still at the hotel."

"On the contrary." The detective leaned back far enough to open the corner closet, revealing Taylor's canvas grip. The bag should have still been back at the *pension* where he and the others had spent the previous night.

Taylor forced himself upright and eased his legs over the side of the bed. He stifled a groan as he pushed himself to his feet and tottered over. He gave the bag a frantic search and came up with his money belt. Which was very strange, since he had left it in the little hotel's front safe. "How did this get here?"

"There, you see? Many questions without answers, just as I said. Your two friends, they race into the hotel; they grab their belongings; they flee. No word to anyone. The hotel manager enters the room; he finds your bag still there. You do not return. He contacts us. We check the safe." He showed Taylor open palms. "So now we are giving you the information you request, Monsieur Knox. All we ask is the same in return."

Taylor handed over his passport. "I don't know anything."

The policeman tut-tutted in the manner of an overly precise schoolteacher. "This is not *Gunsmoke* country. We do not appreciate people who pretend they are in cowboy land."

"I just came here to surf."

The cop had a heavily seamed face and dark eyes that revealed nothing. "You will forgive me for not believing you, Monsieur. But I have never met a surfer before who carries so much money in cash and traveler's checks."

Taylor eased himself back onto the bed, testing each joint in turn. "It's a long story."

"Perhaps you came to France after drugs?"

"What? No!"

"Or perhaps you have already sold your drugs, then stopped for a surf before departing. Did you upset your clients, Monsieur Knox?"

"This is crazy."

"I agree. Most absurd. You will not mind if we take your fingerprints and pass them through Interpol?"

"Do I have any choice?"

"Yes, of course. But I assure you, this hospital is far more comfortable than the back rooms of our police station."

"Take my prints, then. I don't have anything to hide."

"We will see." He motioned his partner forward. Taylor permitted each finger to be inked and rolled across the form. The policeman slipped a small digital camera from his pocket and took several pictures. Taylor started to object, then decided it was far better to comply. The detective scrutinized him with an intensity that suggested he would have liked to peel back Taylor's skull and peer inside.

The detective did not speak again until he was standing by the door. He slipped on his stiff cap and touched two fingers to the rim. "*Adieu,* Monsieur Knox. We will talk again."

chapter 1 4

OVER DINNER, TAYLOR PONDERED WHAT THE POLICE
had said. His entire body ached, yet he could sense a gradual
improvement just since waking that afternoon. He donned his
bathrobe and walked back and forth in the hallway. The hospital staff offered professional smiles and the watchful gazes of
those who knew the police were interested in him.

He returned to his room and bed. The small television attached
to the wall offered nothing save French channels which he could
not understand. He shut it off, turned over, and closed his eyes.

There was no telling how long he slept before the dream arrived. Taylor awoke and rose from the bed in one continuous motion, from sleep to his feet in a heartbeat or less. He stood in the darkened room and searched the night, wondering if somehow the dream had followed him into wakefulness. But the room was empty of all except shadows.

When he returned from the bathroom, Taylor was tempted to ring for the nurse. But he did not want another pill. He merely sought something to help push away the night. His last dream still whispered to him, turning his heart to the same bruised pulp as his body.

He had dreamed he was back with Kirra. Or rather, that he had never left her side. That none of the bad things had ever happened. He had slept, and found himself so deep in an alternative reality he had awakened and *then* thought he was dreaming.

He and Kirra had been shopping. She had held his arm and chatted gaily. Taylor had no idea what she had been talking about. But the image of her face was a vivid blade that stabbed repeatedly at his heart. They were married; he knew that. They were married and together and just another couple in love. Living the normal life, doing daily things.

Taylor sat on the edge of his bed and punched his fists into the sheets. Why was this happening to him? It wasn't enough that he had almost died? That his entire body felt pulverized? That the police were ready to arrest him as a criminal? That he was trying his best to do the right thing? Why should he be tortured now? Now, when he was stumbling through prayers and trying to remember the words of Brother Jonah and keep the flickering flame alive?

The thought was so compelling he almost heard the words spoken aloud. *Turn away.* Why not? What had all this religious nonsense brought him, except naked exposure to the pains he had spent two years keeping at bay?

He struggled back to his feet and tottered over to the window. Outside was nothing save an empty street and shuttered windows and the silent strangeness of another land. He stared at a yellow streetlight and wished for answers.

If only the dawn would come.

IT WAS THE SLEEPLESSNESS THAT SAVED HIS LIFE.

He stood by the window long enough for time to lose all meaning. The hospital grew increasingly quiet until the only sound came from a neighboring room, the steady peeps of some electronic monitor. Taylor remained lost in yearning and remorse.

Then he heard a quiet click.

He turned to see the door crack open. He readied a soft word, in case the night nurse spoke English and wished to scold him for being up. But the door remained only slightly ajar.

Taylor's gaze shifted to the bed. In the darkness, the rumpled coverlets suggested the shadowy outline of a man sleeping on his side. His legs began to tremble, but he could not say precisely why.

The door opened slightly further. A narrow shadow extended into the room. Even before the image reached the level of his thinking brain, Taylor was already moving. He shoved himself off the back wall and accelerated across the room.

He struck the door with his shoulder. The door slammed upon the gloved hand. Outside his room a man yelled. Something clattered upon the floor. Taylor looked down. Just inside the wedged door lay a pistol with an elongated barrel. It was the first time he had seen a silencer up close.

A violent shove from the door's other side propelled him back. He tottered off balance and almost went down. The door flew open and struck him in the forehead. He bounced off the wall, which was not altogether a bad thing, because it gave him enough purchase to ram himself off the concrete surface and push back.

The only reason the attacker was not able to withstand Taylor's feeble efforts was because Taylor's assault caught him as he was reaching for the gun. The closing door pinned his chest to the doorjamb. There was a grunt and a whuffing breath. But the hand kept scrabbling across the floor.

"Police!" Taylor rammed the door one more time, then did the only thing he could think of, which was to fall bodily over the gun. *"Help! Emergency!"*

The attacker fell on top of Taylor. He powered a series of quick jabs into Taylor's kidneys and ribs with one hand, while the other shoved hard under their bodies, going for the pistol.

"Somebody help!"

A very feminine shriek cut him off. From the hallway came a cry in French. The attacker punched Taylor one more time, then leaped to his feet. Taylor gripped the pistol with both hands and rolled away from the boots that were aiming for his head.

The attacker was roaring now, louder than the screams in the hallway. He tried twice to nail Taylor's head with his heel. Taylor scrambled partially under the bed and managed to fit his finger through the trigger guard and one fist about the grip.

He fired without taking aim.

There was a quiet *whfft* of sound. The bullet whanged off one metal leg of the bed and ricocheted across the room.

The attacker leaped through the doorway. He slammed into the nurse and sent her crashing to the floor. The nurse continued to shriek as the attacker's footsteps thundered down the hall.

Taylor slithered out from beneath the bed. The room smelled of cordite and rage. He limped into the hallway. The nurse was still seated on the floor with her legs splayed and her hair in disarray. He leaned against the hall station and offered her his hand. The nurse looked at him, clearly not recognizing this man in a T-shirt and underwear that stood over her. Then she saw his *other* hand, and the screams grew louder still.

Only then did Taylor realize he was still holding the gun.

"No! It's not mine!" He dropped the pistol onto the nurse's station, stepped away, and pointed down the hall. "It was his! That man's!"

The nurse was shrieking her invectives at him now. He caught only one word.

"Yes, go call the police!" He waved at the door in the opposite direction from which the attacker fled. "Hurry! Tell them it's an emergency!"

Several other doors up and down the hallway were open now. Fearful faces peered out at him. An old man's shaky voice called something. This sound steadied the nurse. She swept the hair from her face and said something back. Another voice queried her. She responded more forcefully, then slithered away from Taylor's outstretched hand and pushed herself to her feet. She pointed at Taylor's doorway and ordered him sternly.

"Bed. Absolutely. I'm on my way." He made for his room, hands up and open to show he had left the gun where it was. The nurse waited until he was well through the doorway before she wrapped the pistol in a gray hospital towel and clenched it to her side. Now that she was the one armed and he was defenseless, she felt able to shout more loudly.

Taylor moved to the bed and made as if to lay back down. "Right. Straight back to bed. You go call the police!"

He waited until her footsteps tapped down the hall and the door sighed shut behind her.

Then he was up and moving. He jammed his legs into his trousers, slipped on his shoes, then bundled the rest of his clothes and jammed them into his bag. The hospital hallway was full of chatter, but there was nothing he could do about that. He raced out of the room and down the hallway as fast as his battered frame would go.

He heard the cries of other patients echoing behind him, which only propelled him faster. He took the same stairs as the attacker, assuming that the man would have had an escape route mapped out in advance. The concrete stairs ended at a metal door that was latched open by a coat hanger wrapped around the outside railing. Taylor heard shouts in the distance but did not turn to look. He bounded down the outside stairs and headed away from the lights and the noise. He raced down a fetid alley, took a turn, crossed a street, ran down another passage, and another. He was forced to halt there and lean against a dirty wall. His ribs and lower body ached horribly from the attacker's fists.

Sirens sounded in the distance. Taylor pushed himself off the wall and began limping away from the noise.

chapter 15

TAYLOR FOUND AN OPEN CAFÉ BY THE OLD TRAIN
station and hunkered into a corner. He was sore and tired, but not
particularly sleepy. From his booth he watched night people come
and go. Most were taciturn and scarred by life, hard-voiced women
and men bearing a week's stubble, their eyes gouged by rough living and uneven regimes. The bartender greeted many with casual
familiarity. A few revelers arrived and tried to lighten the mood, but
soon slunk away. Taylor nursed a coffee and tried to find a position
that did not cause his bruises to ache more than they already did.

His thoughts moved in fruitless circles. Images flitted through his brain, of the attack and the surf and the rifleman, back and forth without real purpose. Taylor found that he could hear the cop's voice very clearly. It fitted well into the night and the café and the patrons. The detective droned in Taylor's head, asking all the same questions as before. Then he began to ask *new* questions. Directing Taylor's thoughts toward specific issues. Ones he could answer, and then those he could not. Yet in response to the tight cop-style questions, Taylor found that the mysteries began to segment themselves, re-forming into components small enough for him to inspect.

He could not see an overall pattern. He did not know the final answer. But by the time dawn began to compete with the streetlights outside the café windows, Taylor knew what he needed to do next.

He walked to the bar and asked, "Do you speak English?"

The bartender pursed his lips and shook his head apologetically.

Taylor pulled five twenty-dollar bills from his pocket. "Can you change this?"

Biarritz was a tourist city. The bartender swept up the money, punched numbers into a calculator, and counted out a stack of euros. Taylor left one bill on the counter. "Telephone to America?"

The bartender nodded and converted the bill to coins. He used a pen to write out the international dialing code on a napkin. Then he pointed Taylor toward the hall leading to the kitchen.

Taylor checked the clock above the coffee machine. Five o'clock French time was eleven at night in Maryland. The bartender was laying out little baskets of fresh croissants and circular containers of hard-boiled eggs. Taylor took one of each and asked, "Can I have an espresso?"

His stomach rebelled against the prospect of more coffee. But he wanted to be fully alert for this conversation. Eating only heightened his aches and fatigue. And his doubts. He desperately needed to trust this woman.

He walked back and dialed Allison's home. When she answered, he said, "I hope this is a good time, because I need whatever you've got for me."

"It's the perfect time," she replied. "I think I'm being watched at the office."

"This is absolutely not good news, Allison."

"Do you want what I have or not?"

"Yes. But not if it means getting you hurt." Even so, Taylor found his concerns eased by her own tight tone. This was not the sound of a woman playing both sides. "What do you have?"

"Geneco Labs, remember them?"

"Revell's newest acquisition. Besides us."

"Right. They're about to complete stage-three trials with a new drug. They have kept everything confined to their lab and one wing of a neighboring university's teaching hospital. Very hush-hush. But word is leaking out. The whole company is buzzing. It wasn't hard to catch rumors. It was hard to find two that matched. But I think I have it now."

"Allison, I don't like this at *all*."

"I don't know what's real right now, okay? But Gowers was down four times yesterday, asking if I'd spoken to you, what I knew."

"He knows we've been talking."

"Seems that way. Do you want the rest?"

"Yes."

"Geneco Labs is working on a new painkiller. A derivative of one of their top-selling anesthesias, reformulated as a tablet. It's supposed to be almost as strong as morphine. It has shown to be effective against migraines, cancer pain, heart ailments, severe back injuries, the list just goes on and on. Apparently the side effects are minimal."

"It isn't habit forming?"

"According to what my pet techies have discovered, there are no addictive qualities at all. Revell is using its muscle to push for OTC approval."

The largest segment of over-the-counter drug sales was pain relief. If Revell had a handle on a new painkiller, one able to handle chronic pains without side effects or addiction, they could corner the market.

"What about the standard warnings—fatigue, blurred vision, impaired thinking?"

"Apparently this product is completely problem free. You take it, your pain goes away. Six hours later, you dose up again. End of story."

"They'll make a fortune."

"They need to. Apparently Geneco Labs knew exactly what they had on their hands, and they held out for the moon. They have stripped Revell right down to the bones."

He had what he needed. He knew this in his gut. What precisely it all meant, he couldn't say. Not yet. But that would come.

"Allison, I want you to take that vacation."

"I told you—"

"Listen to me. You've done a tremendous job here. But I need to know you're safe before I can go forward with this."

"What if you need me?"

Something in the tone lodged deep inside his chest. "Allison, you are a real friend."

Allison instantly sensed the change. "I'd like to be. That and more."

"I want you to think about your daughter. What would she do if something happened to you?"

"All right. If you really think I should, I'll go."

"Don't contact the office until you're somewhere safe. Tell them your daughter had an emergency."

"You'll call me?"

"Yes. All right."

"In two days. Otherwise I'll worry myself to death."

"Sure. Allison . . ."

"What?"

"Thank you. For everything."

Taylor hung up the phone. He took several breaths and refocused upon the strengthening day. Then he dug the paper from his pocket and placed the next call.

"OUI, ALLÔ?"

"Mrs. Dupin, this is Taylor Knox. I stopped by your house a couple of days ago."

"It is very early, Monsieur."

"I know. I waited as long . . . is your husband back?"

"He is in the mountains. I explained this."

"I'm sorry, I don't know how . . ." He swallowed hard. "Mrs. Dupin, I think your husband may be in danger."

"Comment?"

"Is there some way you could get word to him? Tell him some people are tracking Kirra Revell. If she is with him, tell her to leave *now*. They tried to kill me last night."

There was only silence on the other end. Taylor added, "This is very real, Mrs. Dupin."

"Where are you speaking from?"

"That doesn't—"

"Please to tell me, Monsieur."

He read the café's name off the license framed by the kitchen door. "Bistro de la Gare, in Biarritz."

"Remain where you are."

"But—"

"Do as I say, Monsieur. *À bientôt.*"

chapter 16

A HALF-HOUR LATER, THREE YOUNG MEN ENTERED the café. Two remained by the door as the third greeted the bartender then moved straight for Taylor. "You are the man who called my mother?"

"Yes." He started to rise but was halted by a slight hand motion by the young man.

"Your name?"

"Taylor Knox."

He was shorter than Taylor, dark and lean and hard as

corded iron. "Last night you ran from the hospital and left your gun?"

"It wasn't mine. But yes, I took off after somebody tried to shoot me."

"So you bring troubles into my land and my family. Why is this?"

The words were softly veiled, but Taylor could feel tension radiating from the man. "I'm not sure yet. But I'm beginning to work it out."

"Perhaps you should go and never return." Compressed energy turned softly sibilant words into a deadly threat. "Perhaps you should never have come."

"They would have found her some other way. It was only a matter of time."

"Ah. Now you are speaking of Kirra, yes?"

The simple word, the easy manner, the glitter deep in the black gaze—something struck Taylor with the force of absolute certainty. This man was in love with Kirra. "Yes."

"You brought them to her, so now they kill you?"

"They try. They must assume the search is almost over and they don't need me anymore."

"Maybe you are the threat and not them. Perhaps I should do the work for them. Maybe then we will all be left in peace, yes?"

"No. I'm not the threat here."

"But I think you are. I think you are a danger to me, to

my family, and to Kirra. So tell me now why I should believe you."

This much he had worked out in advance of the young man's arrival. "There were two men who traveled with me from England. Surfers. The police think they fled to Spain."

"You wish to find them?"

"If I can, I'm pretty sure they can confirm what's going on here."

Reluctantly the Frenchman conceded, "There are three places in Spain very famous for big waves. All of them are in the Basque country."

"These two men were with me at Guethary three days ago."

"I can ask my friends. Their names?"

"Kenny Dean, an Englishman. Red Harris, an American." He described them both. "They're driving a white Ford Econo-line van with British plates. I don't remember the entire number, but it started with the letter *E*."

The young man walked to the bar and returned with a pad and pen. "You will write down their names and this van." He took the paper and walked to where his friends stood by the door. One accepted the note, cast a dark look in Taylor's direction, then departed.

The young man pulled out a cell phone, punched in a number, and began talking at length. He was clearly arguing with someone.

Finally he slapped the phone shut and stalked back. "We go."

"Where?"

"No questions." He was openly angry. "Perhaps you wish to have more discussions with the police? No? *Bon.* Then you stand and you walk and we go. Now."

THEY TOOK HIM TO AS REMOTE A LOCATION AS COULD BE found in a land crowded by sunshine and tourists and good French flavors. A steep-sided valley grew from the Basque farm-lands, where gentle hills grew steadily more vertical and fun-neled into a tight-fisted wedge. A mixed orchard of pears and apples occupied the final segment of level ground. Nestled back against the rockface were six shacks, occupied only at harvest-time. The tree limbs had been plucked clean and the air was thick with perfume from remnants spilled upon the ground. A clean wind blew down from the heights, bearing the chill of semipermanent snow and a winter yet to come.

The young man's name was Inyakie, and he was Basque to his bones. Taylor recognized the same hidden depths he had known in many of his parents' generation, another race too stubborn to ever give in willingly to the march of so-called progress. Inyakie only spoke with Taylor because he was ordered to do so. Taylor assumed the instructions had come from his mother. On their journey to the hideaway, they stopped by the Dupin farm. The old woman had inspected Taylor somberly from her front doorstep, ignoring her son's tirades and arm sweeps as he gathered up provisions. Taylor had waved his thanks before the car pulled back down the drive. The woman responded by returning to her home and shutting the door.

The cabin was clean enough and utterly bare. There was a kerosene lantern, a box of matches, a chair, a single bed, a pitcher, a cup, a plate, a knife, a spoon. A tiny waterfall delivered ice-cold water from the heights. A latrine stood at the orchard's far end.

Taylor slept through the afternoon and much of the night. He awoke ravenous and so sore every movement brought agony. His ribs and kidneys ached where the attacker had pounded him. His head thudded at three different spots. One shoulder hurt so he wondered if his collarbone had suffered a hairline fracture. Even his legs remained weak from tearing down the Biarritz streets.

They had left him a basket of food: a wedge of white sheep's cheese and home-baked bread and apple spread and an onion so sweet he could gnaw on it like fruit. When he was filled to bursting, he cut off the lantern and drew the chair out front of the cabin. He wrapped himself in the blankets and stared out at the night. A pair of nighthawks circled far overhead, singing their cry to the dark earth. The wind was mostly blocked from his perch, but he could hear how the orchard's other side was wrenched by a rising storm.

Sometime before dawn he returned to his bed, as prepared for rest as he could ever be. The gathering storm sang him to sleep.

chapter 1 7

HE WAS AWAKENED BY FOOTSTEPS. TAYLOR TUM-
bled from the bed. Inyakie pushed open the cabin door and
observed him wincing as he rose upright. "You are wounded?"

"Just bruised."

Inyakie carried another basket of provisions in one hand and
a clay pitcher in the other. He set down the food, tore the wrap-
ping off the top of the pitcher, then poured a cupful. "Drink."

"What is it?"

"I told you. No questions. Drink."

Inyakie pretended not to be watching as Taylor took a tentative sip. But when Taylor jerked in surprise, the young Frenchman leaned back against the wall to observe openly. "Drink it all."

Taylor did so. It was not effervescent. But it felt as though bubbles cascaded over his tongue and rolled down his throat. A sense of brightness and well-being spread out through his frame.

Inyakie filled the cup a second time. "Again."

He did as he was told, but more slowly. There was little flavor, just that of any herbal brew. Gradually the pain in his head and limbs began to diminish. Taylor was observing himself intently now. He detected no side effects, no dullness, no rising fatigue. The pains were not eradicated, as was the intent of most modern medicines. They did not completely vanish. Instead, they eased back to a point where they really did not matter so much anymore.

Inyakie pulled a tin from his pocket, unscrewed the top, and dabbed some onto a cloth. He passed it over. "Bathe your wounds."

Taylor smelled the cloth. The odor was very intense yet not unpleasant, a distillation of what he had been drinking. Inyakie watched but did not object as he touched the cloth to the tip of his tongue. His tongue went completely numb. The lack of sensation spread to the inside of his mouth with his saliva. Taylor dabbed the spots on his head, lifted his shirt, and gingerly passed the cloth over his kidneys and collarbone and lower ribs. Gradually the pain diminished to a mere afterthought.

"This elixir aids the healing as well as reduces pain?"

"I told you, no questions."

But there was no question anymore. "This is what Kirra was after. Why she came."

Black fire shot from Inyakie's gaze. "I do not like the sound of her name in your mouth."

Taylor nodded slowly. Oh yes. He knew.

Inyakie called out the open doorway. The same man who had guarded the café's door entered the cabin, his hands full of clothes that he dumped on the chair. Inyakie said, "Dress in these. Bring the food. We must hurry."

"Why?"

This time he chose to answer. "We have found your two friends."

THEY TOOK A SMUGGLER'S ROUTE INTO SPAIN. TAYLOR wore the local clothing of white collarless shirt, oversized Basque beret, red kerchief, and black drawstring canvas pants. They traveled in a worker's van the color of dried mud. The van was stacked with boards and surf gear. Neither Inyakie nor his stocky companion spoke to Taylor. The road was scarcely more than a gravel track. Stretches had been paved, but so long ago the asphalt was ground by time and weather to grassy rubble. A misty rain drifted in the windless air. They wound through an increasingly high pass, through forests of wild cherry and alpine fir so ancient they formed a solid canopy overhead. Twice they confronted other vehicles careening straight toward them. Both times they pulled so close to the edge rocks tumbled over the cliffside. The two men in the front seats seemed utterly unconcerned by the closeness of oblivion. Instead they leaned out the window and traded jolly insults with the passersby, speaking in a rough-hewn tongue that could only have been Basque.

Taylor found that he did not mind the isolation. There was much to think over and digest. Certainly the temptation was there to hate the man before him, one who would gladly feed him to the uniformed lions. Yet time after time his mind returned to Brother Jonah's final words. The *restricted* path. The *narrow* way.

When they emerged from the woodlands, they passed through a veil of cloud and rain and emerged into brilliant sunlight. They crossed a highland valley beneath a blue-black sky. Through the open windows spun an icy fragrance that made a mockery of lowland life. The van jounced and bounded over a heavily rutted track. To either side, cattle lowed. A pair of stone huts stood upon a rise, from which the occupants could survey the entire vale. A man appeared in one doorway and shouted something lost to the distance and the cattle. A word from Inyakie and the driver swerved off the track and headed for the cabin.

The man hefted a rifle from the doorjamb, slung it naturally over one shoulder, and came down to meet them. He easily weighed more than the three of them combined. Inyakie bounded from the van before it halted and exchanged a two-handed clasp so fierce his beret spun from his head. He scooped up his hat and scolded the sun-blasted farmer. The giant merely laughed and walked over to peer into the van. He caught sight of Taylor and boomed at him as well. Inyakie answered curtly.

The man pointed to the boards behind Taylor and switched to severely fractured English. "What you doing, hey? You think maybe we hide ocean up here? You like to surf on my lake?"

"I'm just following orders," Taylor replied.

The man gave off a pungent odor of unwashed clothes, hard work, and cattle. "Big mistake, mister. These boys, they dumb as my cows." He pointed north. "The sea, she is that way."

Inyakie was not pleased by the herdsman's sociability toward Taylor. He spoke at length, but the giant merely grinned harder. He unslung his rifle and shook it in front of the windshield. In his grip the weapon looked like a matchstick. "Sure, we're friendly peoples. The bad mens come; we give big welcome; they stay long time."

Taylor leaned forward so as to speak directly through the window to Inyakie. "You're expecting somebody?"

Inyakie shook the giant's hand, then reentered the car. The giant backed off and bellowed a farewell. Even his voice was oversized, scarcely contained by the valley. The driver honked his way through the lowing cattle and rejoined the track.

Taylor waited until they started their descent to try one more time. "Do you think we're being followed?"

This time Inyakie responded. "Somebody is watching my family's house."

"Who?"

"A professional." He turned far enough around to glare darkly. "You have brought danger upon my family."

Taylor felt remorse as deep as pain. "Should we have left your mother there in the house alone?"

At this the driver snorted, the first sign that he even understood English. Inyakie replied to the windshield, "My mother is Basque. She lives in the village where her mother's mother's mother was born. She is never alone."

THE VILLAGE OF MUNDAKA WAS THE MOST BEAUTIFUL place Taylor had ever seen.

North of the French border lay four Basque counties, two of mountains and two of the sea. Spain possessed four times that number. The interior country was filled with hardscrabble villages of rock and closed-faced folk. Clouds locked steep-sided Pyrenees valleys in permanent gloom. Even the thickest woodlands were monochrome. As they approached the ocean, the cities became larger and the landscape grew scarred. Towering smokestacks added inhuman shades to the gloaming overhead. Apartment buildings conquered the hills and traffic clogged the highways. There was neither logic nor beauty to the sprawl.

They turned off the highway and passed through Guernica, the city Franco had bombed to rubble in his futile attempt to vanquish the Basque spirit. Past the city, the sun finally reemerged. They took an elm-shaded lane over a series of descending hills. They finally entered a narrow defile of grass and bleating sheep and a meandering river.

The river broadened into a slow-moving basin. Trees swayed a lazy summer welcome. The gorge expanded into a pair of emerald arms. Where the river joined the sea, two narrow islands rose like forested jewels. An ancient village perched on the last fragment of flatland between the cliffs and the sea. In the stone-lined harbor, fishing boats sparkled. Time was not welcome here, nor the world's great woes.

Even from this distance, Taylor could see the waves. They glistened in the sunlight like streaming crystal pipes.

As they followed the road paralleling the river, Inyakie placed a call on his cell phone. Whatever he heard caused him to point the driver into the village's heart. They parked in the square behind the church. Two other Basque men were there to greet them. They were dressed in identical garb and stood by a pile of surf gear. Taylor watched as Inyakie and the driver rose to greet them. Through his open window, he heard the sound of liquid thunder.

The Basque stared in his direction. Taylor could not help

but wonder at his own response. He was by nature not a passive man. His standard answer to any foe was battle. Yet here he sat, willing to simply accept and move on. He could not say why. He had traveled half the world around, met the man in love with the woman who had held his heart captive for so long, and felt nothing. Not anger, not jealousy, not humiliation. A trace of sorrow, a vague hope that Kirra would not feel the same about Inyakie. But not even much of this. None of it made any sense. Yet for the first time since the wounds had been reopened, he felt able to live with himself.

Inyakie waved him over. Taylor rose from the car and joined them. The locals gave him a flat gaze and a murmured greeting. Inyakie said something to them in Basque. One of the men motioned for Taylor and Inyakie to follow him. They took a cobblestone lane away from the church, passed through a village market, and halted at the border of a larger parking area.

Taylor spotted the vehicle immediately. "That's it."

Inyakie asked, "You are certain?"

"I lived in that van for a week. That is Kenny's van."

Inyakie said something in Basque, then, "We go."

"Where?"

"Come."

There was nothing to be gained from arguing. Taylor followed him back to the car. To his surprise, Inyakie and the driver began pulling their gear from the back. "We're going for a surf?"

"We are going for answers." Inyakie tossed him a wet suit. "How do you feel?"

"A little sore, but okay."

He handed Taylor a battered thermos. "Two cups. And remember. This eases the pain. But your body is still not healed."

"I'll be careful."

They suited up, grabbed the boards, and headed toward the thunder. Two blocks over they entered the harbor area. A crowd gathered on the far sea wall. Two ice-cream salesmen were surrounded by children. People strolled and clustered and pointed out to sea, enjoying the waterborne theater.

Taylor followed the others down a series of seaweed-covered stairs. He launched himself into the water between two moored trawlers. The air was thick with the scent of exposed shellfish and of nets drying overhead. His entire body tingled with the second dose of elixir.

They paddled to the harbor entrance and halted. A new set was crashing against the islands, blowing spume high into the air. The sound was of a single constant explosion. A dozen or so surfers jockeyed for the outside position. The crowd shouted and pointed in anticipation. The waves re-formed, reduced by the islands from suicidal proportions to barely manageable heights. The first wave arrived, a surfer took off, and flew, and flew, and flew. The waves were not as large as Guethary, but they held to the most perfect shape Taylor had ever seen. The surrounding cliffs blocked all wind. The sea was mirror-flat until the next wave rose like a giant clothed in streaming blue. Call them twenty-foot faces. The lip pushed out very far, forming a tunnel large enough for a bus to drive through.

The set's final wave blasted into froth and din. Taylor was ready when the others started paddling out. The water still rocked slightly from the undercurrents stirred up by the waves. Otherwise there was no disturbance. They covered the two hundred feet easily. When he reached the lineup, he understood why there were not more surfers in the water. These were, after all, perfect waves. But from this angle the sea wall rose almost close enough to touch. A wipeout meant being mashed against the rock. The exposed barnacles glistened like fist-sized black teeth. A surfer would have to be utterly confident of his or her ability to make the wave. Fear, uncertainty, the slightest instability was a death sentence.

Then he spotted Kenny. "There!"

Red was the first to see him coming. His face clenched taut and he said something to his companion. Kenny turned and gasped aloud.

It was all the confirmation Taylor required.

The Brit tried to greet him with an amiable grin. "Taylor, mate, how're things?"

"Save it." He paddled around to the outside, so that Kenny had to put his back toward the other surfers. "I want to know what happened."

"Hey, it's a magical day. Did you see my last—"

"Maybe you didn't hear me." He shifted over close enough to grip the nose of Kenny's board. "Tell me how we hooked up in Scotland."

Kenny watched with mounting alarm as the four Basque surfers clustered in tight. "Are these mates of yours?"

Taylor saw Red trying to ease away. "That's the other one. Don't let him go."

Kenny's eyes widened as Inyakie barked a command, and instantly one of the others gripped Red's leash and pulled him back. "What's going on here?"

"Take a good look at the sea wall," Taylor said. "Ask yourself how well you want to get to know it."

"Look, mate, I was the one who saved your life, remember?"

"That's the only reason we're not asking harder."

The Brit's semipermanent tan could not hide his blanched fear. "I didn't sign up for any assassination. Straight up."

"Let me help. You were approached by some guys in Scotland. All they wanted was a little information. Find the American surfer staying at Iona, try to discover where he's headed." He took Kenny's silence for affirmation. "When I came back and asked you for a ride south, it must have seemed like a gold mine had just opened up at your feet. They'd given you a contact number. You called; you said you'd do it for cash. How much did they pay you, Kenny?"

"You've thought this one through," Kenny grudgingly acknowledged.

"How much?"

"A thousand pounds. You know how hard I've worked for a thousand quid?"

"So you played me like a fool."

"Hey, all I knew was, you were on the run. Not even the monks on Iona wanted you hanging about, right?"

Kenny's eyes flickered seaward. Behind Taylor came the booming rush of the next set striking the islands. Kenny's speech accelerated. "When you took that last wave at Guethary, I spotted the shooter up on the cliff. And I knew it was a lot more serious than you running from the law. I couldn't have that, mate. I don't care what you did. Nobody deserves to go out like that. So I did what I could. I got you to shore. I went running up the path, screaming like a banshee, armed with nothing but a board with a dent in the rail. A couple of locals were shouting over from that little park; they saw me and headed over as well. The shooter started to aim my way. I tell you, I thought I was a goner. Then he took off. I guess he decided there were too many of us by that point to take us all down. I hung around until the police showed up with the ambulance. Then I scarpered. The last thing I needed was a run-in with the Frog coppers."

The set's first wave lifted them up a swooping ledge of danger. "So how did you get your money?"

"Look, mate, I've told you all—"

"You met up with them once we got down here. You had to."

"I don't know what you're talking about."

Inyakie swooped in from Kenny's other side. "Maybe we just push you over the ledge, see if your friend is any more helpful when he sees you screaming and bleeding on the wall."

Red's shriek was almost feminine. "I don't know *anything!*"

Taylor accused him, "You were there."

"I *wasn't!*"

"Shut up, Red."

"Not when it mattered! He wouldn't let me come. I got two hundred pounds and sat in the *van.* He went to the meet by himself!"

"But you took the money."

"Yeah, but—"

"Enough!" Inyakie motioned to his mates. "You took a portion of this blood money. You helped place my family in danger."

"Inyakie, no."

"Let this coward see what the Basque call justice."

"Don't!" Taylor gripped the arm of Kenny's wet suit and shouted to be heard over the roar of the breaking waves. "Talk while you still can!"

"I figured the house and that old woman was what they were after." Kenny's cry was almost as high-pitched as Red's. "So I wouldn't tell them until they delivered."

"Tell me what they looked like."

"Two men! One was a Yank, tall, gray haired, didn't talk much. The other was a Brit. Ex-cop."

"How do you know?"

"I've seen my share of coppers, okay? I had a run-in for bringing in some weed, did six months. This guy knew it and knew how to use it." He was pleading now, shooting glances at Taylor, at Inyakie, at waves that had suddenly become menacing. "He was going to have his mates on the force find me carrying and send me up. Do you hear what I'm saying? I had no choice!"

"Enough." Inyakie motioned to his mates. "Say your farewells."

"*No!*" Taylor paddled so that he was now between the Basque and the pair. "Don't do this!"

"He has threatened my family! He must pay!"

"Is this the way you want to start with Kirra?"

That halted the Basque. "What?"

"I know all about tainting a relationship. You do this, you will regret it for the rest of your life!" When Inyakie tried to move around him, Taylor shoved him back. "Listen to me! It doesn't matter whether you're right. Do you hear what I'm saying? *It doesn't matter!*"

The set's final wave crashed and pummeled the wall, then subsided into a frothy hiss. Then silence. The sea was utterly calm. Inyakie sat upon his board, so close Taylor could see the sea salt upon his lashes. "What do you say?"

"You do this and you'll have lost the chance, and it will be your fault, and you will have to live with this for the rest of your life." Taylor felt hollowed from an argument that had suddenly become a confession. "Kirra's more important than revenge. Let them go."

Inyakie did not speak, nor move.

Taylor said to Kenny, "You and Red get out of here. Paddle through the harbor, get in your van, leave Spain, and never return."

When Red slipped prone onto his board, one of the other Basque said something. Inyakie did not respond.

"Hurry," Taylor said.

The next set was bearing down upon the islands by the time Kenny rounded the harbor wall. Only when both surfers disappeared from view did Inyakie speak. "What did you mean by that?"

But Taylor was all done talking. "Figure it out for yourself."

Before the Basque could respond, Taylor proned and paddled away as hard as his bruised muscles would permit. The first wave had re-formed inside the islands and was bearing down fast. He saw a couple of others going for it but powered determinedly forward. Taylor glanced behind him, ignored Inyakie's glare, and aimed for the peak. The two others jockeying for position realized Taylor had the inside track and eased off. Taylor did not so much want the wave as he wanted to be away. His body was already complaining from the strain. But his bitter frustration granted him the necessary punch to mount the crest, slide over the lip, rise to his feet, and fly.

All Mundaka waves broke from right to left, flowing down

the length of the river mouth and weakening as they went. Because Taylor surfed with his left foot forward, his stance was with his back to a left-breaking wave. The wave jacked up fast and hard, going vertical with shocking speed. He pointed straight down and took a heart-stopping slide along the face of a liquid mountain. At the base he carved a long deep turn, flying at such a tight angle his right shoulder almost touched the water, and threw a fantail out toward the observers along the sea wall.

He drew in tight to the face and mounted back up slightly, crouching as he did so. He twisted slightly and reached forward so as to rest his right hand on the inside railing, and trailed his left hand on the wave face. It was a classic tube-riding stance. Only now the sound of the wave breaking behind him was being reflected by the sea wall. The bellow was deafening and hit at him from all sides. It was impossible to tell how close behind him the wave was breaking. The temptation was to punch down harder on his front foot, accelerating out beyond the wave and the danger and the crushing wall. But Taylor was not after safety.

There was no conscious thought behind his actions. Time elongated upon a wave, and deliberation ceased. The intensity of surfing large waves was fiercely possessive. Taylor's response was an action drawn from his core. He stomped down on his rear foot, shifting all his weight back toward the fins. He could sense the board slowing. He could hear the heightened roar, feel the rush of wind being blasted from the boiling nucleus. The echo off the sea wall shrieked danger. And he simply did not care.

The curtain descended. The outer wall was so thick the light diminished to blue shadows. The wave bellowed and blasted him with spume. He shook his eyes clear and focused on the tunnel sweeping up and around him, and on the swatch of green and blue up ahead.

The wave spat him out. He was flying so fast he crested the diminishing lip and did a full 360, rotating around his back fin before slipping down the wave again and aiming for the shore. The wave released him in an easy sigh. He fell to the board and began paddling for the beach beyond the village's border.

Only then did he hear the cheering.

Taylor glanced to his right. The villagers lining the sea wall were applauding and laughing and shouting his way. He sat up on his board, astonished.

People of all ages, most dressed in the Basque homespun, delighted in one man's fearless moment.

There was only one thing he could do. Taylor grinned and waved in reply.

He paddled to the shore, walked up to dry land, and seated himself facing seaward. Beauty surrounded him on all sides. He felt replete for the first time since the attack at Guethary. He raised his face to the sun and closed his eyes. His heart felt not so much wounded by the revelation he had shouted into

Inyakie's face as cleansed. He had no idea why. Nor could he say how he felt both hollowed and sated. But he did. For the moment, the sensation alone was enough. He shook his head to a few simple words carried upon a sea gull's cry.

The narrow way.

WHEN THEY RETURNED TAYLOR TO THE CABIN BY
the orchard, he asked Inyakie if he could use the cell phone.
The young Basque hesitated only a moment. "I don't need to
warn you."

"No," Taylor agreed. "You don't."

The ride had been long and tiring. But there had been
none of the tension that had accompanied them on the way
out. Several times Inyakie had turned in his seat, as though
wanting to ask Taylor something. But the words had not

come. Taylor had seen the indecision in the man's eyes and said nothing. For the moment, it was enough not to be despised.

When Inyakie passed over the phone, Taylor felt more explanation was required. "I promised a friend I would check in."

"A woman?"

Taylor hesitated. To agree was to say far more than he wished. "A friend."

Inyakie showed the first glimmer of humor since their meeting. "I am very glad to hear this, just the same."

Taylor walked out among the trees before placing the call. Allison answered on the first ring. "I was hoping it was you!"

"I promised I'd call."

"Don't tell me you always do what you say. I'd have to lock you up."

A final glimmer of daylight lanced between the high peaks, turning the orchard into a cathedral of shimmering green. "It's good to hear your voice, Allison."

"Do you know, this is the first time since all this started that I don't hear the distrust in your voice."

"It's true." He knew it was also dangerous. And he didn't care. Not just then.

"Why the change?"

What to say? "There's a woman I'd like you to meet sometime. Ada Folley. When I was a kid, she tried to tell me about some things, but I was just too dumb to listen." He could hear her now. Whispering across the miles and the years. Oh yes. Be ready.

"Taylor?"

"Sorry. It's been a long day. Ada used to say you know a person's worth by the choices he makes. Today, right now, I want to trust you. Is that a good choice?"

"It is to me."

"You've changed too."

"Have I?"

"This is the first time I'm not hearing any of that coldness you use. The first time in—"

"Years. Too long. It's harder to trust than I'd like to admit."

"I know."

"But it's nice to have a reason."

"I'm not nearly as perfect as you'd like me to be," he said.

"I'm not after perfect. I'm after a reason to trust."

"I don't even know how to give a woman that much." He reached up to trace a design along the lowest leaves. "You know what makes you so special?"

"I'm not, Taylor. But tell me anyway."

"You've been handed a raw deal from the beginning. You could write a book of excuses for living on acid and hate. But you don't."

"I couldn't and still be the mom I want to be for my little girl."

"See? That's what I mean. You're there for the ones who

need you. You are the most reliable assistant I've ever known. You do your very best to be a great mom. You live with an open heart and gratitude." He kicked at a piece of overripe fruit. "You humble me."

"Stop."

"I'll just say this and nothing more. I've lived a life marked by too many wrong choices. I've been an expert at justifying my actions. And I hate myself for doing it. Worse, I hate the pain I've caused those stupid enough to love me. I want to change, Allison. I don't know if I can, but I want to."

The sun dipped behind the cliffs. The air took on a crystalline quality. The world seemed caught in an eternal moment between lightness and dark. Even the wind stilled. Taylor observed himself, a man of muscled strength and human frailty standing in an orchard beyond time and space, an Eden made holy by defiant hope.

He realized Allison had not responded. "Are you there?"

The voice was scarcely more than a whisper. "Yes."

"What's the matter?"

"You shouldn't talk to me that way. Some doors hurt too much to open, unless they're really open." She took a shaky breath. "Where are you now?"

"France. You?"

"Someplace a lot less exotic. My aunt's. I've never been anywhere. What is France like?"

He looked down the long row of trees to where Inyakie

sat on the cabin stoop and chatted quietly with his friend. "Confusing. But getting clearer all the time."

THE NEXT MORNING INYAKIE ARRIVED ALONE. HE SET down a fresh set of clothes along with the day's food. "How do you feel?"

"Better."

"You have taken the elixir?"

"Not since last night."

"Drink just one cup this morning."

Taylor did as he was instructed. "You are a healer like your father?"

"Not like my father. No one is like him."

Taylor found flaky croissants in the basket, still warm from the oven, and homemade preserves. "Why aren't you up in the hills with him?"

"Kirra wanted . . ." Inyakie halted in midstride. The Basque flipped his beret in his hands and stared out the window at the gathering day. "She has gone into the hills with him."

Taylor tore off another bite of the croissant. "Your English is excellent."

"I studied biochemistry in Bordeaux. Afterward I did three months' research in America."

"Where?"

"Boston."

"It's cold up there."

"Yes." He twirled the beret by the rim. "About Kirra."

Taylor dropped the remainder of his croissant back into the basket. "You love her."

The stubby fingers, brown as the earth outside the open door, flipped the beret so fast it blurred.

"Does she love you?"

"I have asked her to marry me."

The realization pushed Taylor back against the wall. "That's why she went up into the mountains alone, isn't it?"

"Not alone."

"Without you. She went up because she needed time to think this through."

"And then you show up." The sun pouring through the doorway cast his face into shadows, all but the glimmer in his dark eyes. "Bringing danger and woe."

"But that's not what we're talking about," Taylor said, meeting the smaller man's gaze. "Is it?"

Inyakie flipped his hat onto his head and rose to his feet. "I think it would have been better for us all if you had never come."

TAYLOR DID NOT REALIZE IT WAS SUNDAY UNTIL THEY pulled into the village of Sarre and heard the ringing church bells.

Sarre was a typical Basque mountain village, all whitewashed walls and red shutters and winding narrow lanes. The people bore expressions as tightly enclosed as the surrounding mountains. Taylor followed Inyakie through the church's outer wall to discover not a courtyard, but rather a graveled cemetery. The wall opened into the town's central square, which meant the graves lay at the heart of the village. They were tightly massed and so adorned with flowers it was impossible to read many of the headstones.

The church's interior was whitewashed simplicity. Time-blackened wood formed the pews and pillars and circular balcony stairs. Inyakie led him to a middle pew where his mother sat alone, her head covered by a woven black veil. She cast Taylor a single look, neither welcoming nor hostile, then slid over to make room. Inyakie turned and walked away.

Other than the priest and a few children, Taylor was the only male in the congregation. He found this vaguely disappointing. He did not expect a chamber filled with other male seekers. But it would have been nice to feel a little less alone. The priest began the service, and Taylor followed the example of those around him. Within a few moments he realized the priest repeated everything first in French and then in Basque. Taylor found an odd comfort in both the practiced manner of their Sabbath worship and the fact that he understood nothing. There was time here for reflection upon the unsaid.

His time with Kirra was over. He knew that with utter certainty. Kirra had a beautiful woman's ability to deflect male admirers. She would have allowed Inyakie's feelings to progress to this point only if she felt deeply herself. And she could not feel for this man while still holding any real affection for Taylor.

His circuitous thoughts were halted by the first song. The ancient church was utterly filled with voices. *Male* voices. He turned and stared upward. A balcony ran all the way across the back of the church and extended into two broad arms that ran over halfway down both sides. The gallery was *filled* with men. They stood in uniformed ranks, every one of them dressed in standard Basque garb. They did not sing the words. They *shouted*. They cried out in plainsong, their harmonies deep-throated and booming. There was no musical accompaniment. None was needed. The church seemed hardly large enough to contain their voices.

Mrs. Dupin caught his astonishment and smiled slightly. She rolled her eyes, as though to say the men were showing off again. Taylor disagreed entirely. He loved this. He wanted to be up there with them. He felt the power of their worship in his chest. The final word of each verse diminished to a long droned note as though the men were reluctant to let it go, as though they found an abiding reverence in the power of song.

When the priest began his message, Taylor returned to his internal dialogue. How did he feel about Inyakie being in love with Kirra? The answer was the same as it had been these past three days. He felt helpless. Utterly and completely helpless.

It was the same response he had known since beginning this

search. Only now there was one crucial difference. No longer was he driven by a desire to regain what he had lost. He could not explain it any better than that. When the congregation rose to its feet and the next song began, Taylor remained seated with his eyes closed. He needed to understand this. Of course he hurt still for Kirra and the mistakes he had made. But the pain no longer controlled. Of course he wanted her. But his life was not dominated by this.

In all the time since he had wreaked havoc in both their lives, he had never before been able to accept things as they were.

Part of him wanted to renew the struggle, to regain control. Taylor shook his head at this temptation. Two years of thrashing about had brought nothing but more pain. He had no choice but to look ahead. What lay before him he could not say. But one thing was absolutely certain. The thought was etched as clearly into the air before his closed eyes as the music that surrounded him.

He was no longer alone.

AFTER CHURCH HE DISTANCED HIMSELF FROM MRS. Dupin and strolled to the cemetery's far end. The dispersing congregation drifted through the market square in the communion of generations. Families took tables at the restaurants and cafés shaded beneath vine-clad verandas. Taylor continued around the cemetery walk until he was alone with the distant green hills. If only there were some way to leave the past and the tumult behind. To feel and think as clearly out here in the light of day as he had inside.

He heard the scrabble of footsteps on the gravel walk behind him. But he did not turn around. Whoever it was, this person would bring back the problems of the day and his unfinished business here. He sought a way to bury his internal commotion. Just lay it down, place his own tombstone over a whole world of mistakes, and walk away.

Instead, the past walked over and spun him around.

Kirra was dressed in a mannish outfit of brushed trousers with a tightly cinched waist, a khaki shirt, hiking boots, and a deerskin vest. She looked as lovely as he had imagined. All but her expression, which was furious.

She hauled back and struck him square across the face.

chapter 1 9

THERE WAS ENOUGH ENGLISH IN KIRRA'S BLOW
to draw tears from his eyes. Taylor wiped the back of his hand
across the inflamed patch. Her eyes blazed as she reared back
for a second blow. Taylor flinched, but neither resisted nor
tried to defend himself.

"No." Inyakie moved forward and gripped the hand before
it could strike. "Enough."

Kirra struggled to free herself. "How *dare* you show up
here!"

"This is not the place for blows," Inyakie told her, gripping her more tightly. "Nor the proper day."

Since her hands were trapped, she spat the words at Taylor. "Haven't you done enough damage already?"

"Amanda said you had left a message asking for me."

"And you *believed* her?"

"At first," he admitted. "Initially I did."

"You of all people should know Amanda can *never* be trusted."

"Yes. You're right."

"Then why—"

"Because I wanted to believe her. I wanted to think you still wanted me." He grimaced an apology as much to Inyakie as Kirra. "I was a fool."

Kirra shifted slightly, enough for Inyakie to accept she was under control again. "You've endangered this family, my work, everything."

"If Amanda hadn't sent me, she would have used somebody else. But she *would* have found you, Kirra. What you're doing here is too critical for her to just leave alone."

Her eyes tightened. It was a new expression, this gaze of glinting fury. What hurt worse than the distrust in her features was the knowledge that he had done a great deal to put it there.

She said, "You have no idea what I'm after here."

"You're wrong."

"You can't possibly—"

"Kirra, I know about the product Amanda's secretly bringing to market. I know she can't afford to let you continue your research. I know Revell's on a financial knife's edge. I know they have to succeed with this new pain medicine. I know you're a threat to everything."

"How do you know about Amanda's new product?"

"Enough," Inyakie repeated. "Here is not the place for such secrets. Besides, my father is waiting."

Kirra evidently wanted to stab Taylor with her finger. "He doesn't deserve to come within a hundred miles of Jacques Dupin."

"Perhaps. But my father has asked for him. So we go. Now."

INYAKIE DROVE THEM IN THE SAME VAN THEY HAD TAKEN to Spain the previous day. Kirra fumed in silence. They wove along a forested road, through farmland and hamlets, then turned onto an unmarked trail that took them straight toward the nearest cliffside. Taylor caught sight of something in the trees just after the turning. He swiveled about and spotted a Basque man crossing the trail behind them, rifle slung over one shoulder.

When he turned back, he saw that Inyakie was watching him in the rearview mirror. "My father is much loved," he said simply.

"I don't mean harm to any of you," Taylor replied.

Kirra exclaimed, "Then you should *never* have come!"

"I told you. If it wasn't me, it would have been another. At least I'm trying to be on your side."

Inyakie surprised them all by saying, "I believe him."

"That's because you don't know him like I do."

Inyakie pulled up between a pair of trees whose trunks were thicker than the van. He cut the motor and said, "Perhaps it would be a good thing to leave your anger here."

"Did you hear anything I've just said? This man is a danger to us all!"

Inyakie rose from the van, opened the rear door, handed Taylor a backpack, gave Kirra a second, and shouldered the largest himself. "What if he is right? You yourself have said how Amanda is so . . . what is the word?"

"Tenacious," Taylor offered. "Immoral. Competitive. Combative. Vicious when crossed or cornered. The most dangerous opponent I have ever met."

Inyakie eyed him. "And still you believed her?"

"Only because I hoped that Kirra was still in love with me."

Dark eyes showed fathomless depths. "And now?"

Taylor replied to Kirra directly. "Amanda had me kidnapped and trapped inside the Spanish fortress, knowing it would tax me to the limit to escape. She shot up her own library just to make sure the message got through, that I believed someone else was out to find and kill you. She orchestrated two teams to follow me. When she discovered where you had been headed, she arranged to have me killed.

Do you really think she would have left you alone if I hadn't agreed to help? She *has* to find you. She has to *stop* you."

Inyakie nodded slowly. He had heard the unspoken message. "You have a plan."

"I think so."

"Come, then. My father must hear this also." Inyakie disappeared around a jink in the trail. "We will let him decide."

THE CAVE'S MOUTH WAS THIRTY FEET TALL AND HALF again as broad. Just inside the shadows, the temperature dropped twenty degrees. They passed from summer heat to constant chill in the space of three steps. Inyakie exchanged halloos with two armed men stationed on a high overhang. He then moved toward a rocky alcove where an old man and a woman with a fretting baby sat upon a ledge fashioned like a bench. A pair of lanterns glowed overhead. Another lit the interior of a half-hidden alcove. Inyakie slipped the beret from his head and stood at the alcove's entrance, waiting.

Kirra used their relative isolation to hiss, "I would never have come back to you. Never in a million years."

"I knew that the instant I met Inyakie." Taylor swept a hand to encompass the two men on guard duty, the cave, the watchful locals. "All this didn't just happen because I showed up. You were *ready*. You were *expecting* something. You *knew* Amanda was coming after you."

"And you let her use you."

"Guilty as charged." He did his best to ignore the attention of everyone else within the cave. "I'm here. Nothing can be done about that. But maybe I can help to make things better."

Her laugh echoed through rocky depths far beyond the lanterns' reach. "You've spent years underestimating my sister. You have no idea how demented she is over getting her own way."

"I know when she couldn't break us apart any other way, she hired detectives to take—"

"You know *nothing*. Amanda hired a prostitute to seduce you."

He was forced back a step. "What?"

"That woman you met on the beach? I hired my own detectives, showed them those horrid photographs Amanda gave me, and tracked the woman down. She was *paid*. Bought and paid for by my sister." The pain tore her own words to shreds. "That was when I knew Amanda had to be punished. Hurt where it would hurt her the most. Stopped from doing to more people what she's done to me."

Taylor faced the watching locals as he would judge and jury. Kirra looked out to sunlight and the empty forest. "It doesn't change what I did. I destroyed us. And I'm sorry. I'll carry that regret to my grave."

He watched her ire dissolve a notch. "How am I supposed to stay angry with you when you talk like that?"

"I'd do anything to replay that portion of my life."

"Well, you can't. It's done, destroyed, over. And it's your fault."

Approaching footsteps forced them apart. Inyakie pointed back to the lantern-lit alcove and said, "My father will see you now."

JACQUES DUPIN HAD A PRESENCE FAR GREATER THAN HIS height. He was not much taller than his wife, scarcely rising higher than the base of Taylor's rib cage. But he was broad and solid as the surrounding rock walls, with eyes that glowed more fiercely than the alcove's lantern. His hand was stubby and rigid, his grip fierce. He continued to hold Taylor's hand as his gaze slipped away and came to rest upon Kirra. He studied her a long moment, nodding slightly. Then he turned to Inyakie and said something. The younger man immediately left the alcove and spoke with the people seated upon the stone bench.

Jacques still did not release Taylor's hand. He spoke again, this time to Kirra. She clearly disliked his request. Jacques spoke again. Reluctantly she said, "Jacques says he hasn't used his English in years and wants me to stay and translate."

Taylor had the distinct impression the healer wanted to make sure Kirra was listening. "Fine with me."

Jacques led Taylor over to a table and two chairs. The cavern was full of medicinal gear, herbs, a portable sterilizer, two battery-operated halogens, a gas-powered stove, metal water cistern, and a case of empty glass jars. The lantern softened the cavern's jagged edges and sealed the opening in shadows. The healer's hands probed about the wounds on Taylor's head.

"He asks how you were injured."

"The older one happened before I left Florida. The other was when a shooter tried to take me out at Guethary." He winced as Jacques traced a hand over the stitches.

Kirra examined him for a long moment, then translated. "He says you should please tell him the full story."

Taylor did so, watching as Jacques withdrew scissors and tweezers from their sterilized packets. Kirra translated, "He asks why the hospital did not remove the stitches."

"I had to leave there in a hurry." Taylor ignored the tugging on his scalp as best he could by watching Kirra's worried expression. The lantern added an ethereal glow to her skin. She was not his, had not been for years. But her beauty could not be denied, nor her appeal. Studying her from this proximity left him hollowed and wounded anew.

"Explain, please."

After Taylor recounted the second attempted assassination, the healer motioned for Taylor to ease off his shirt. He spent a long time examining Taylor's torso. "Jacques asks if your legs are also injured."

"A couple of bruises."

"Do your joints ache?"

"Some. Not bad, considering."

Jacques took a yellowish salve that smelled of crushed flowers and applied it to Taylor's ribs and bruises. He talked as he worked. Kirra translated, "The Basque culture was born in a time beyond time. Napoleon finally conquered us, the last provinces to be brought into France. In punishment for our desire to live free, the Basque were forbidden education. We were banned from all universities. Our language was outlawed. We were refused passports. We were treated as nonpersons, denied all chance of advancement. This prohibition lasted for 143 years."

He had Taylor lean over so as to treat his back and continued, "Up to the Second World War, there was only one hospital in the entire French Basqueland. It was located in Bayonne. This was a two-day journey from the Basque capital of Saint Jean Pied de Port. Most doctors working in the Basqueland had been ordered there by Paris. Many came as punishment for incompetence and addictions and thievery. Most of these doctors spoke no Basque. The Basque spoke little or no French. The doctors often hated the place and the people. The locals called the Bayonne hospital the Hotel of Death."

"I've heard about the Basque terrorists fighting for nationhood."

"That is a small minority of our people. Most, including myself, disagree both with their actions and their aims. Times have changed. We are too small in numbers to exist as a nation alone. Spain and France now recognize our heritage and help us preserve our language and our culture."

Jacques handed Taylor his shirt. From the neighboring alcove, Inyakie ushered out the old man and motioned the woman forward. Taylor realized that the son was acting as healer in the place of his father. Jacques continued through Kirra: "In earlier times, however, the situation was very different. The church was the only place where the Basque might come and hear their language and receive instruction. The church maintained records of medieval herbal remedies and helped pass this knowledge on from one generation to the next. Even after the repression ended, still the healers remain a respected part of the Basque culture. Only now our work is illegal. The medical establishment considers us a throwback to an era of witchcraft and sorcery. But we Basque are used to holding things in tight secrecy. Healers do not advertise. We seek out no patients. Our names appear on no registry. To the outside world, we do not exist."

Inyakie entered the alcove long enough to collect two bags of dried herbs. He gave them to the woman who carried her child, bid them farewell, then returned to the alcove where his father worked. Kirra moved to stand beside him. Inyakie locked gazes with Taylor as he drew Kirra close.

The old healer turned to study the pair, his son and the lithe American woman. When he spoke, Kirra's gaze grew wounded. She did not speak. The silence was complete. Taylor listened to the lantern's stutter and waited.

Finally Inyakie translated, "My father reminds Kirra that she also brought this danger to our doorstep."

"Not intentionally," Taylor replied.

"My father says she must move beyond her guilt and her regret, if she is to forge a new future. She must release the past. Just as you should do."

Taylor's mouth worked hard to form the words: "I don't know how."

Jacques began nodding with his entire body, as though deeply satisfied with the response. Inyakie continued to translate, "Faith is not a single step. Spiritual growth does not end with the initial turning. First you learn to trust God. Then He leads you to the next stage. And the next. And the one after that."

The healer drew his chair around so that Taylor could see him and, at the same time, beyond his shoulder, the couple holding each other in the doorway. Jacques spoke, and the translation came from behind him. "Do you truly wish to leave the past behind? Do you want to grow *beyond* where you stand today?"

Taylor nodded not so much from agreement as realization. He had never found release from the past because he wanted to keep it as much as he wanted to let it go.

Jacques formed a fist between their faces, so tight his arm corded. Inyakie translated, "How we struggle and fight to do what only love can accomplish."

Then he blew upon his fingers, poof. And the hand relaxed. The hand and the fingers and the arm. And he spoke in English for the first time. "So easy, yes?" He rose and clapped Taylor on the back. "Come. We will eat and you will tell us of your plan."

chapter 20

THEIR DISCUSSION TOOK THE BETTER PART OF three hours. Taylor emerged from the cave to find the surrounding forest a realm of slanted gold and looming shadows. Behind him the cave was filling with people Inyakie had telephoned. Taylor felt drained from the exertion of thinking and plotting, all done under the somber gaze of a woman he had once thought his own. During the meeting, Kirra had never moved from her place by the opposite wall, close to Inyakie and as far from Taylor as she could remain.

The force of her gaze had been as exhausting as the discussions.

He carried Inyakie's phone and did as the young Basque had instructed, climbing to an elevated position above the tree line. But when he arrived upon the rocky outcrop, he left the phone in his pocket. Instead he just sat and surveyed this world of forested mountains.

"Taylor?"

"Up here." He remained where he was and watched Kirra climb toward him. "Have they already decided?"

"They'll be hours yet." She huffed herself up the last incline. "Nothing fast happens in this world."

He watched her select a rock several paces removed. "I can see why you love it here."

"Can you?"

"The people are as genuine as any I've ever met."

"They remind me of the old Minorcans back home."

"Not to mention that it's as far as you can get from the Revell lifestyle and still remain on this planet."

She tossed a rock toward the setting sun. "There's a lot to be said for that."

He pulled his gaze away from her and took in the snow-capped horizon. "And this place is as beautiful as anywhere I've ever seen."

She threw another rock, brushed off her hands, and said very deliberately, "I want to apologize."

"There's no need."

"I wasn't talking about today."

"No," Taylor quietly agreed. "I wasn't either."

She rose to her feet, hesitated, then asked quietly, "Why are you doing this, Taylor?"

A rook chuckled at them from a neighboring tree. High overhead a hawk swept graceful curves through the sunset. Taylor replied, "The whole time we were together, it was me first, us second. I never let go of my pride or my rage or my stupid selfish . . ."

He stopped. The sunset bathed her in gold, strong as a halo. "I want to do something for you, Kirra. For *you*. I can't explain it any better than that."

Kirra stood a long moment gazing down at him. Then she reached over and placed a hand upon his cheek. She left it there for a time, then turned and walked back down the rise.

Taylor watched her disappear into the forest. He felt her touch on his face, as strong as God's own benediction.

He waited until her footsteps had merged into the sibilant hush of forested dusk. Then he dialed the number from memory.

Allison answered on the first ring. "I don't have anything important to say," Taylor said in greeting. "I just wanted to hear your voice."

"That's important enough for me."

"Would you mind if we just talked for a while? Not about work or what's going on. Just talk."

"I'd like that," she replied. "So very, very much."

chapter 21

THE RAINS SETTLED IN JUST AFTER SUNSET. TAYLOR spent the night lying in his bedroll, listening to the deluge, and running the plan through his mind. The cave was dry enough, and the chill was offset by a pair of fires kept banked and roaring through the night. But the rain whispered to him of flaws he had failed to uncover. He finally flipped his coverlet aside and went to sit at the cave's entrance. It all seemed so futile now. How could he ever have expected to take on the might of Revell? He sat for hours, chased by the fiends of doubt, fearing he heard heaven's tears splashing outside the cave.

Inyakie found him there sometime after midnight. "Are you ready?"

It was far too late for false confidence. "I have no idea."

"My father says the man who plans well never sleeps well. Come."

Taylor balked at the guns slung from the three men's shoulders. "We don't need those."

"Let us hope you are correct." Inyakie disappeared into the rain.

The drive back to Biarritz took two long and silent hours. They wound through empty streets and parked by the entrance of a third-rate hotel. A figure in a rain-slick anorak emerged from a doorway and slipped into the rear seat beside Taylor. Only when he flipped back the hood did Taylor recognize the senior policeman from the hospital.

The cop said in greeting, "I told you we would speak again, did I not?" He shook hands with the three Basque, spoke softly in their tongue for a time, then returned his attention to Taylor. "Inyakie is a friend. His father saved my father's life. These are the only reasons you are not in chains, Monsieur Knox."

Taylor responded with a tight nod.

"So. I am to understand you have an explanation for why I am sitting here tonight?"

"Such talk is for later," Inyakie replied.

"And now you are directing my movements?"

"We asked for help," Inyakie said.

"So I am here. But before we move further, I must know why this is happening."

Taylor halted Inyakie's protests by saying, "I came here looking for an American woman. Her name is Kirra Revell. Her family controls one of the world's largest pharmaceutical companies. Kirra has been on the trail of an ancient herbal remedy that threatens to destroy the market for a new Revell product. This market is worth billions to Revell."

"This is one of Monsieur Jacques' remedies?"

"Yes."

"Then why," the cop demanded of Inyakie, "did Monsieur Jacques not send this American lady on her way?"

Inyakie responded by studying the rain drumming on the car hood.

Taylor replied, "Things get a little complicated at this point."

"And they were simple before?" But the cop was smiling. "This American lady, she is beautiful?"

"Very."

"And young?"

"Enough about Kirra," Inyakie said. "It is late and there is much to be done."

The cop asked Taylor, "So these men who tried to kill you, they have followed you here?"

"If they're who we think they are."

"Remind me again why we are assuming you are not part of the threat, Monsieur Knox."

"They shot at me in the water, remember? They tried again in the hospital."

"But only," the cop reminded him, "because you brought them here."

"If Taylor had not come, they would have sent another. At least he has a plan." This from Inyakie. "Enough with the questions. Enough."

"Bon." The cop nodded. "A plan. I am listening."

Taylor sketched out his idea once more. But the night and the rain and the cop's unblinking intensity muted his confidence. He listened to himself and heard only the possible weaknesses, only the chances for failure.

When he stopped talking, the policeman sat in silence and studied him. Taylor readied himself for a professional's objections. But the cop merely said, "Two men. One British, one American. The American is Jackson Yerby. Tall, gray haired, eyes like smoke. The British carries himself like a professional."

"We're told he's a former cop." Taylor was suddenly very alert.

"His name is Colin Tomlinson." The cop had difficulty with both names. "The car spotted by the Dupin residence is rented by the American. The hotel rooms are both billed to his credit card. These names mean something?"

"No."

He handed over two passports. "Do you recognize either of these men?"

"The shooter on the cliff was too far away. The hospital room was too dark to see anything." Even so, Taylor studied the passport photos intently. He tried to compare the American's to a man in sunglasses driving a Caddy along the road from the Jacksonville airport to St. Augustine. But that had been a million miles ago. "Sorry. I'm drawing a blank."

The cop retrieved the passports and tapped them on his leg. He spoke tersely to Inyakie in Basque. Inyakie replied in English. "I believe him."

The cop slipped the passports back into his pocket. "I have spoken with the hotel manager. These men have had visitors. Four, perhaps five men. All are, how do you say, hard cases, yes? Very hard cases. One we believe is a local. A pro. You understand?"

"Yes."

"Very well. We will tap their phones and set a wire in both rooms."

"And their car."

"The car. Yes. More of a problem but we will see what can be done. When do you lay your trap?"

"We have spread the word for two days from now. We leave at noon."

"Then I must be busy, yes?" He moved for the door, then stopped. "Monsieur Knox, you will come and report to me the remainder of your story when this is done. Inyakie, you will bid your father a hello from me, yes? And tell him to take great care."

THEY ARRIVED BACK AT THE CAVE SOMETIME BEFORE dawn. The next thing Taylor knew, Inyakie was shaking his shoulder and settling a steaming cup by his head. Taylor pushed himself upright. The cave was a hive of activity. Inyakie said, "We depart in ten minutes."

Beyond the cave's entrance, sunlight turned every dripping surface into a prism. They drove a battered old van and an equally derelict Citroën. Taylor, Inyakie, and Kirra sat in the car and watched Jacques bid his wife a fond farewell and slip into the van's front seat.

The village of Sarre greeted them with flags and bunting. The autumn festival marked the end of summer, when the cattle were brought down from the summer highland pastures. An off-key village band practiced the national anthem. The market square was full of locals covering trestle tables with starched linen and heaping piles of food. A trio of spits roasted two hogs and an entire sheep over banked coal fires. A pair of wooden kegs taller than a man were rolled to either side of the central fountain and chinked into place. A group of old men were seated on the fountain's edge, holding glasses of wine so red they looked black in the sunlight. They toasted Taylor's convoy with raised glasses and toothless grins.

Midway up the mountain lane, they were forced to halt and pull aside. The road ahead was filled with lowing cattle and barking dogs and whistling herders. The cattle were curried until their coats gleamed. Ribbons had been woven into their tails and manes. Garlands of fresh wildflowers were wrapped about their horns. Taylor spotted the herdsman they had seen in the highland valley. Inyakie rose from the car and held a hurried conversation with his friend. The grinning giant shouted something that was lost to the cattle's din and waved them on their way.

Inyakie said to no one in particular, "In an hour the whole world will know of our departure."

They entered the highland valley and parked their van by the now empty herder huts. The young man driving the Citroën spun the car around and headed back for the lowlands. Besides Inyakie, Kirra, and Jacques Dupin, they were accompanied by four others, two men and two women, all experienced at harvesting medicinal herbs. Since many of these plants were known to live in just one or two highland valleys, it was vital that the pickers leave enough for the plants to grow new shoots.

Once they checked their accommodations, they shouldered their packs, crossed the valley, and took a narrow path up and over the western ridge. Although Jacques was the eldest of the group, he set a pace that had the rest of them puffing and struggling to keep up.

Inyakie eased back so that he walked alongside Taylor. The air was rarified enough to leave them both winded. The night's rain had cleared the air such that flowers to either side of the path seemed etched from skyborne colors. They walked in companionable silence for a time, then Inyakie asked, "You have Basque heritage?"

"No. Minorcan."

"This was perhaps once a Basque tribe?"

"Not to my knowledge."

Kirra spotted them walking together, and her pace momentarily faltered. Then she hurried to catch up with Jacques. Inyakie waited until she had vanished around a jink in the path to say, "This plan of yours. It is good."

"I hope you're right."

"We have centuries of experience fighting stronger foes. Last night, my father said your plan was very Basque."

"That's the finest compliment I've heard in a long time. Please thank him for me."

They crested the ridge. Patches of snow hugged the permanent shadows cast by several rock overhangs. Although it was still summer below, the wind was a breath of highland winter upon Taylor's face. Ahead of them stretched a highland vale, untouched by man or machine. From this height, the narrow basin was a fingerlet of brilliant green. Other than this single path, there was no way in or out. No house stood there, no road, no tree, no sign of man.

Together the two of them turned to look back over the way they had just come. The world stretched into a panorama of diminishing hills and majestic pastels.

Inyakie stood beside him, taking draughts of the sweet air. "Kirra has agreed to marry me."

The light dimmed. But only momentarily. "Congratulations."

Dark eyes forced their way under his skin. "You are not angry?"

The day was too piercing and heaven too close for anything other than the truth. "It is tempting. But it would lead nowhere."

Inyakie nodded slowly. "The time has come to make our ancient remedies known to the outside world. I have prayed for years, asking God to bring me a way. When Kirra arrived, I knew it was the divine hand at work. But then you came, and I thought . . ."

The silence was enough to finish the statement. Taylor said quietly, "I understand."

"We Basque are known for blood feuds that can last for generations."

"The Minorcans also."

"My blood calls for us to be enemies. But my spirit says otherwise. I have seen you with my mother, my friends, my father. I have seen you in my church, and seen your own search for the divine hand. I have seen you keep me from doing great harm to another at Mundaka." He gazed over craggy mountains descending to emerald-clad hills. "I cannot love my God and hold to this anger against you."

"Nor can I."

"It would taint my love for Kirra as well. As you said in the Mundaka waters, it may even destroy us."

The wind's fingers pried a single tear from Taylor's eye. He blinked it away.

"Truly, now." Inyakie offered his hand. "You believe we can be friends?"

There was only one answer he could give. Taylor accepted the iron-hard grip and replied, "With God's help."

From far ahead, Jacques hallooed, urging them to hurry. As they started along the path, Inyakie clapped Taylor's shoulder and said, "It is a *very* good plan."

chapter 22

THE TEAM DIVIDED THEIR TIME BETWEEN THE hidden valley and the herdsmen's huts. There was no source of water in the hidden valley. Which was why the herders did not use it for their cattle, that and the difficult access. The small valley where they worked was accessible only by the long trail snaking over the razor-edged ridgeline. Each dusk Jacques and his little crew hiked back to the herders' cabins in the broader valley directly east. Because the surrounding peaks were so steep, the hidden valley lost light around three in the afternoon.

Direct sunlight was required to identify any blooming herbs, because the plants rolled up their flowers each afternoon as protection against the coming cold.

And cold it most certainly became. By the time they hiked over the ridgeline and arrived back at the cabin, they could see their breath. The huts' one nod to modernity was an oil-fired stove. The herders drove up an oil tank each summer and took it down before the first snows. Each dusk, Jacques fired a stove and made a pot of pungent herbs. They took their mugs out to watch the dimming light.

Sunsets were lingering affairs. The western reaches became crowned with streamers that turned simple stone into celestial peaks. There was no ambient light, nor people, nor noise. Even the softest whisper became an interruption to the orchestral display. When the first star appeared, they trooped back indoors for the evening meal. Watches were set, bedrolls spread, and all but the first guard were swiftly asleep.

By the fourth morning, Taylor was beginning to fear he had judged the situation entirely wrong.

They awoke to yet another cloudless dawn. Taylor had volunteered for the predawn watch, the longest of the night. It was his duty to stoke the stove and fill the pots with fresh water and prepare the morning coffee. The oil tank was almost empty, so in the evenings they let the flame go out. By morning the cabin and their bedrolls were frosted white. The lake and streams had begun to grow ice edges at night. Before the light had grown strong enough for Taylor to cut off the lantern, the others were stirring. He sweetened the mugs with condensed milk and set them by each head, allowing the others to warm their bones before fully emerging.

After breakfast, Taylor filled a basin with steaming water and took it into the neighboring cabin designated for the men's ablutions. He was not sleeping particularly well. The longer they stayed up there, the more he was convicted by how Kirra and Inyakie acted together. The intimate looks, the quiet smiles, the glow that outshone the lantern each night, the quick touches, the way she would rest her hand upon his shoulder or slip into his embrace as they watched the sunsets. All of this weighed heavily.

Kirra softened around Inyakie in a way she never had around Taylor. In return, Inyakie was chivalrous. His decorum was almost formal. Each night Taylor sat in the corner he had claimed as his own and saw how Inyakie had become her knight. He was strong for her, patient with her. His passion was a flame, yet he made no demands of Kirra. It shamed Taylor so bitterly that he felt as though his insides had been scooped out and burned over their cooking fire.

The truth was obvious. This was Kirra at her best. And it was far finer than she had ever been with him. To see them together was a harsh reminder of just how wrong he had been. How desperate he was to be better. How fearful he was of being unable to change.

Taylor finished shaving and stood watching the gathering light when Inyakie entered. The young Basque tossed him a backpack filled with the day's provisions and announced, "We go."

Taylor followed him from the cabin. They took up position behind the others trudging up the steep path. "Today we're through?"

"Jacques says we have been here long enough."

Taylor mulled that over as they trekked upward. "Which means I've failed."

"You weren't wrong."

"We brought up eight people to pick plants at the backside of nowhere. There are more people guarding your house. The cop has planted wires and tapped phones. Nothing's happened, and I'm not wrong?"

"You're tired because you've been on watch."

"I'm fine. I just don't see how you can say I wasn't totally crazy to suggest we do this."

Inyakie halted by the final switchback before they crested the ridge. He took a couple of breaths so as to speak more easily. "The people who watched my house were pros. I told you that. The policeman agrees. Your plan was good and you were not wrong."

Ahead of them, the man on lead pointed back down the pathway and yelled, *"Ils arrivent!"*

Taylor did not need to know what the man had said. The alarm on everyone's face was more than enough. He dropped to the earth. Inyakie scrambled up the path at a crouch and flattened beside Kirra.

Below them, figures in camouflage backed away from the first cabin. There was a drumming compression in the air about him. The cabin lifted off its foundations from the power of the explosion. Flames burst from the door and window and around the eaves.

Kirra cried aloud and started to rise. Inyakie halted her with a hiss and a fierce grip.

"I count six," Taylor said. "No, seven."

"Too many," the man beside him agreed.

"The cabins," Kirra moaned. "Our things."

"Our lives," Inyakie responded. "Stay down."

One young man eased the rifle from his shoulder and slid the bolt. Jacques yelled sharply. The man whined and gestured at the attackers. Inyakie added his voice to that of his father's. Dejectedly the guard rammed his gun into the dust beside him.

Four of the hunters had spread out, automatic rifles at the ready. They stared up to where Taylor and his party cowered. "Get ready to run," Taylor said.

Attackers moved to the other cabins. There were further *crumps* as one by one the huts went up in flames.

Two of the hunters checked through the van. They fanned their rifles and blasted the rear windows. But this was not enough. They emptied their clips into the van, riddling it with bullets.

Inyakie managed to keep to a semblance of calm. "Do you recognize them?"

"I can't see their faces."

"Kirra?"

But she was weeping too hard to see anything at all.

The attackers pulled the sacks of gathered herbs from the demolished van and tossed them into the nearest burning cabin.

Jacques tensed and spoke a warning. Taylor had seen it as well. "They're coming!"

The attackers' movements distinguished them as seasoned professionals. Two of the hunters moved out to either side. The others started up the path behind those on point. All of them held their weapons at the ready.

"Quick now," Inyakie said, hefting Kirra to her feet.

They slid to the ridgeline's other side and scrambled northward. Behind them came a shout of alarm. As soon as Taylor slipped below the line of sight, he moved up to take Kirra's sack. She was sobbing heavily and moaning her sister's name. Taylor tossed the pack to the next man in line, gripped Kirra's other arm, and helped Inyakie accelerate them to greater speed. The going was very uneven. The altitude robbed them all of breath. By the time they had covered a quarter-mile all of them were huffing and stumbling.

A rifle shot rang out behind them. A bullet whanged to Taylor's right. A puff of dust and a white scar marked the earth's wound. Nobody said anything. They could not spare the breath.

Jacques was by far the most nimble, despite his age. He bounded ahead, rounded a corner, then came back to wave them forward. They passed the outcrop to spy a cave's mouth up ahead. They staggered forward and into the gloomy depths. Taylor and Inyakie dropped Kirra to the dusty earth and returned to the mouth. Taylor's heart hammered so hard he could see the tremors in his hands where they gripped the rock. His mouth gaped, his lungs heaved, yet he could not seem to find breath.

The first of the hunters came around the bend. Inyakie took one of the rifles, aimed carefully, and fired. The bullet careened off a rock by the attacker's head. The man ducked back behind the first rock.

One of the others futilely tried his cell phone, then stowed it away. There was no signal anywhere in the valley.

They waited through the pressure of gathering silence. Kirra rose and wiped her face and stood behind Inyakie. There was no sound.

Kirra asked for them all, "Why aren't they coming for us?"

Taylor said, "They weren't after us to begin with."

"But they shot at us."

"No, they didn't."

"If they had aimed for us, they would have hit us," Inyakie agreed.

"Then what—"

"They were herding us."

"Why?"

"They were only after the herbs."

A half-hour passed. Nothing happened except for a strengthening of the daylight beyond their cave.

Then they smelled the smoke.

Kirra said, "That can't still be the cabins."

Taylor and Inyakie exchanged a glance. Jacques merely shook his head and turned away.

"Can it?"

A sudden burst of wind balled the smoke up like a fist and shoved it through the cave's mouth. They all backed up coughing.

Taylor demanded, "Is it true what Jacques said, the herbs grow in just one valley?"

"It is known to all in this region," Inyakie confirmed. "Almost every valley is a different microclimate."

Kirra cried, "Somebody tell me what is going *on* here!"

Jacques said to his son, "Go and make sure."

Since Jacques had spoken in English, Taylor took it as an indirect order and followed Inyakie from the cave.

They did a quick reccy from the mouth, then scrambled up the rockface and came out on top of a promontory. Inyakie was half a body-length in front of Taylor. He scouted to the west, or tried to, but the smoke was too thick to see anything. Taylor waited through a pair of rolling clouds. When the third arrived, he was already up and moving. Inyakie hissed once, then rose and followed.

Taylor could scarcely see the ground in front of his feet, much less where he was headed. But the smoke was borne up to the ridgeline by slight puffs of wind coming from ahead and slightly to the left. He used the fretful breeze as his only compass and concentrated on keeping upright. The going was trackless and rough.

Suddenly the screen parted, so fast he was caught coughing from the last oily burst. Utterly in the open, Taylor dropped hard.

Inyakie fell alongside him. Softly he repeated, "You were right."

There was no need to respond. Down below them, four men swept the valley from ridge to rocky ridge. They wore metallic packs that glinted sharp in the growing sunlight. Hoses ran down the length of their arms, connected to long pipes which the men held down against the dry autumnal grass as they walked. Fire spouted from the pipes. Flames formed sharp red lines that ran across the valley floor like disorganized ribs. The irritable wind plucked the flames and scattered them in growing ferocity. The smoke was growing increasingly dark and pungent.

Inyakie plucked at his sleeve. "Either we go now or we will never find the cave."

The return was through smoke so thick the sun turned an angry crimson. Taylor's eyes streamed such that he was certain they would have to turn around and retreat above the smoke line. He managed to track behind Inyakie by gripping the man's shirttail. The Basque was far surer in his direction and led them back to where the ridgeline dropped away and the cave mouth reappeared. Taylor lowered himself off the lip and felt arms there to guide him down. He bent over in a ferocious fit of coughing.

Kirra demanded, "Tell me what you saw!"

Inyakie hacked, drank from an offered canteen, coughed again, and reached for Kirra's hand. "Come away from the smoke."

She allowed herself to be pulled further back. "I want to know!"

"You know already." Inyakie gathered her into his arms. "Your sister's men are torching the valley."

THE COP'S NAME WAS LIEUTENANT ARMAND.
Taylor recalled it when he heard Madame Dupin greet
him. He watched the policeman bow over the old woman's
hand with timeless gallantry. Inyakie's mother responded
with the grace of an impish queen. The cop went next to
Jacques and bowed a second time as he shook the healer's
hand. He then made his way around the Dupin kitchen
where they all were gathered, weary and smoke stained
from their trek down the mountain. Armand paused long

over Kirra. He switched to English and said, "Now all has become clear."

"Excuse me?"

"Policemen are known to have strange senses of humor," Inyakie said. "Or none at all."

Kirra shrugged her incomprehension and turned back to the kitchen's side window. Of them all, Kirra remained the most deeply affected by the valley's destruction.

The cop finally made it to where Taylor sat. "It appears your plan has succeeded, Monsieur Knox."

"If they go away, it worked," Taylor corrected.

"They are already gone." Armand accepted a steaming mug from Madame Dupin. "After the attack they crossed directly into Spain. None of them have been seen again. We have alerted the Spanish authorities. Warrants have been issued. But these men are professionals. They know how to disappear."

"Did I not say?" Inyakie asked the room. "This was a very Basque plan."

Kirra cried, "But they destroyed our valley!"

It was Jacques who replied, "It will grow again. We will see to that."

Inyakie took her hand in his. "What Taylor said is correct. The only way we can be certain you are safe is if your sister believes the threat to her company has been erased."

"But—"

He gentled her with his tone. "You trust my father, yes?"

"Of course."

"You heard what he said. Nothing of any great importance grows in that valley. But what would the attackers know of this? The attackers heard we went up to gather the special herbs, the ones that can be picked only at this time each year. They hear this and they find us and they destroy the source. The *only* source. And now they are gone." He stroked her cheek. "So why do you cry?"

Madame Dupin bustled over. "And why must all men be so blind?" She swept Kirra out of her son's arms. "What do you know, you great brute with your talk of plans and sources and I don't know what."

"But, Mama—"

"Did you not hear what she said? Are you deaf as well as blind?" Madame Dupin enveloped Kirra in a huge embrace. "*Our* valley, she said. She weeps because she hurts for *our* land. Can you not see this lady is becoming Basque?"

TAYLOR ARRIVED AT HIS OFFICE IN ANNAPOLIS
hours before anyone else. He watched the techies filter in and
accepted their uncertain hellos. They might never know the
reason, but they were sensitive to the corporate winds. They
knew his fate was sealed. He glanced into Allison's work station, missing her, yet glad she was removed from the tumult.

He did not wait for Gowers to come downstairs. At the
stroke of nine, Taylor entered the chairman's outer office. The
company chief did not keep him waiting long. "I want an
explanation and I want it now!"

Taylor countered with, "Has the merger with Revell gone through?"

"I'm the one asking questions here!"

"Just tell me this one thing. Please."

The CEO glowered over the length of his cluttered desk. "No thanks to you."

Taylor felt the knot of tension he had carried back with him from France begin to ease. "I want something in return."

"You want . . . your job is on the line here!"

"Wrong. I'm already canned."

There was a flicker deep in the CEO's gaze, enough for Taylor to know he had guessed correctly. Gowers lied, "That's yet to be decided."

"Amanda Revell and I have a bad history. I told you that in the chopper out to her boat."

"That's no excuse for running off without a moment's notice!"

"You're not concerned about my absence. You want to know why she ordered me away, and what effect it has on your own future."

The chairman thoroughly disliked having his subordinate taking the upper hand. But there was nothing he could do about it, and they both knew it. "Well?"

"I told you, I'll explain it all, but only if you agree to do this one thing."

"What?"

"Yes or no."

"Yes, all right!"

Taylor did not bother to sit down. He ran through the bare bones, Kirra's disappearance and the lie of a message asking him to come.

"Did you find her?"

"Yes. She's fallen in love with a Basque healer."

"A what?"

"It doesn't matter. She's safe, she's in France, and she's not coming home."

Gowers did not take it well. "Amanda Revell jeopardized the merger just to locate her wayward sister?"

"She is used to having her own way."

"So why . . ." Gowers realized the question was out of line. But too late.

"Why does she still insist you fire me? I told you before. We've got a lot of history."

Gowers lumbered to his feet. Taylor avoided the perfunctory handshake by walking back to the entrance. From that safe distance he said, "Call Amanda. Tell her she owes me. And that I have it all on tape."

"Wait just one—"

"Can't," Taylor said, already out the door. "I've got a plane to catch."

WHEN TAYLOR HALTED BEFORE HIS MOTHER'S HOUSE, HE found Ada Folley weeding the front flower bed. She raised up in stages, stripped off the gloves, and gave him a fierce hug. "How you been?"

"I'm fine."

She released him far enough to inspect his face. "You look it."

"I am. Really."

"Go in and greet your momma. Then come back out here and tell me how is my little girl."

The screen door slapped shut. "I'm here."

Taylor bounded up the front steps. "I'm so sorry, Ma."

"You already told me that on the phone." She brushed aside the apology with a lifetime's practice. "You said it was over."

"That's right, Ma."

"But you lost your job."

"It's okay. Really. I'm thinking of starting a little business on my own." He looked back at Ada. "With Kirra."

"You two back together now?"

"Not now," Taylor replied. "Not ever."

Ada climbed the steps for a closer inspection. "You all right with that?"

"Yes, Miss Ada. I am."

She squinted over his words. "Something's sure different here."

Taylor took a long breath. "I've started listening, Miss Ada."

"Have you, now."

"And praying."

She propped her hands on her hips. "Well, it's way past high time, I can sure tell you that."

"Yes, ma'am. It is."

She smiled for the first time since all this had commenced. "And all God's children said, Amen!"

THIS TIME, HE WAS THE REVELL HELICOPTER'S ONLY passenger.

The chopper landed upon a circular bed of green by the Bethesda Hunt Club, the most exclusive in the nation's capital. A gray-suited corporate gopher held his jacket in place with one hand and his toupee with the other. "Mr. Knox?"

"Yes."

"Ms. Revell is waiting for you." He settled Taylor into the golf cart's passenger seat and headed out.

Amanda's foursome were gathered on the third tee. The other three players were all male. Naturally she played first. She hammered the ball down the fairway, then said, "You guys play on. I'll catch up with you."

The corporate gopher did not wait to be told to back away. She used a rag from her rear pocket to wipe the club. "I ought to use this on your head."

"Your guys already tried that. They failed."

"Threats don't work with me, boyo."

"It wasn't a threat. And you know it. Otherwise we wouldn't be meeting."

Amanda wore wraparound shades that glinted copper and

hard in the sunlight. She slipped behind the wheel. When they pulled down the fairway, she said, "So talk."

"You sent me to find your sister. I found her. You promised me a share of the buyout. I'm here to collect."

"I don't recall—"

"I know about the Geneco Labs pain remedy you're bringing to market. I know about Kirra's research. I have it all down on paper and tape, wrapped with a lovely legal ribbon."

"You can't prove a thing."

"I don't need to. I have your request to send me off. I have the reasons. All I'd need to do is put this in the hands of a half-decent PR firm, and the mess would go prime time. I can see the *48 Hours* special now."

Amanda halted where they were screened by an island of tall firs. "I could shoot you myself right here, and my trained seals would swear I was defending myself."

"My little taped insurance policy says you'll think again." He pulled a CD jewel box from his inside pocket. "The local French cops didn't take kindly to your heavies shooting at me from the cliffside—"

"That is libelous slander!"

"—And trying again in the hospital."

"You don't have a shred of evidence!"

"They tracked me using two traveling surfers. I have their testimony. The cops bugged your men's hotel in Biarritz—"

"Stop trying to tie me to something I know nothing about!"

"Your goons called your cell phone, Amanda. The secret one." Taylor waved the case so the sunlight danced off the CD's mirror surface. "The same number you gave me."

Amanda winced as the light struck her face. "Get that thing away from me."

"This is your copy. Compliments of the house."

"Put it away." She slipped off the kidskin glove and began tapping her diamond ring upon the steering wheel. "I underestimated you, sport."

"Bad move. Very bad."

"So I see." She formed a fist. "All right. Here's how it's going to play. You'll get your cut in the form of a single cash payment."

"Three million dollars."

She actually laughed. "You're insane."

"That's my price."

"Half a mil. And you'll count yourself lucky."

Taylor slid from the carriage. "Pity your new product launch is going to be so badly tainted."

Her fury was such that her features turned splotchy. "Get back in here."

"What for? We're not even talking the same language."

"Get *in*."

"Three million, Amanda. That's what you promised me back on the boat, remember? Or I walk and you suffer the consequences."

She stared out over the empty fairway. "All right. Done."

"I want it in writing. Now."

"I'm not telling you again, Taylor. Sit *down.*"

They drove back to the waiting aide in hostile silence. As soon as she halted, Taylor stood and backed from the cart. He had no interest in remaining close to Amanda Revell for an instant longer than necessary.

She demanded pen and paper from her staffer. She said as she wrote, "This instructs my attorneys to pay you three million dollars for services rendered."

"Have your man witness it."

"Do as he says."

She accepted the paper back from her aide, read it once, then rose from the cart. She stalked to where he stood. "You're never to show your face around here again. Is that clear?"

"Perfectly."

She handed him the paper. "It's cheap at the price. Daddy's disowned Kirra. I get it all. Or perhaps you already heard that from her."

He carefully inspected the document. "Haven't you heard? She's marrying the Frenchman."

"At least she showed a trace of good sense in that move."

Carefully Taylor folded the paper and stowed it in his pocket.

"Daddy was right. That might make you rich, but scum you were and scum you'll remain." Amanda stomped back to the golf cart, slid into the seat, and ordered her aide, "I'm definitely done here. Drive me to the others."

The staffer looked uncertainly toward where Taylor stood. Amanda shrilled, "Forget him. Get in here and *drive!*"

Taylor stood where he was, surrounded by pines and bird-song, and watched her disappear down the slope.

epilogue

Six months later

HE HAD NEVER DREAMED THAT PARIS COULD BE
this expensive.

Taylor kept telling himself that it didn't matter, he could
afford it. But the money seemed to blister his hands as it
slipped away.

Allison could not help but notice his concern. She chose to
wait until they had put Clarissa down for the night to tell him,
"We don't have to stay here."

"Yes we do."

"Taylor—"

"I promised you a honeymoon. I live up to my promises."

Her smiles were coming more fully now, even when they were arguing. She had not smiled much at the beginning. Even after she had learned to trust him, to accept his word as his bond, to know he was determined to give her the best of everything at his disposal, still she bore her emotional wounds. Taylor had no objections, or if he did, he chose not to express them. After all, he was still in the process of learning his own lessons of letting go and moving on. She knew this too and granted him a whole heart load of latitude.

Still, when she smiled as she did now, with a heart full of love, with her gaze and all her face shining, he could cry with the joy of knowing there was a thing called hope after all.

She asked, "Do you really think I need a place this fancy?"

The words sounded feeble even before they were fully formed. "I want to give you something special."

Their courtship had been a series of carefully measured steps, and unlike anything Taylor would have ever scripted for himself. Which, if truth be known, was one reason he was so certain it had been both right and divinely ordained. They had spent weeks finding a church together, for one thing. The three of them would talk all week about the last one visited and the next to come. They decided by joining a new couples' class in a church where Clarissa discovered she loved to sing. Allison's little girl carried her own set of scars. Taylor counted it as a star-flecked blessing to hear the little girl sing. For him.

They had a room under the eaves of the Hotel Intercontinental on the Rue de Rivoli. The room was long enough to be called a mini-suite. The balcony doors were open, and they were seated on the sofa, nestling together under a quilt they had dragged over from the bed. Clarissa was asleep on a trundle bed in a small adjoining room. Outside the balcony doors, Paris was slowly settling under a blanket of midnight snow. The Eiffel Tower flickered in and out of sight, framed by spotlights and snow, floating in the night.

Allison might have chuckled, or perhaps it was merely a sigh. She said something to herself.

"What?"

She nestled into his neck. "Nothing."

"We can afford this."

She kissed his face. "Are you telling me or yourself?"

"Don't do that."

"What, this?"

"I'm serious."

"You're always serious. You're the only man who takes his wife to Paris on a honeymoon, then spends his time talking to lawyers."

"I've got a lot to do before I see them."

"Do you still leave tomorrow?"

"Last I heard." He knew it was futile. But he needed to say it once more. "Come with me, Allison."

Her only reply was to kiss his neck.

"Why not?"

"Because this is something you need to do on your own. And you know it." She snuggled in closer. "But thank you for asking."

The next morning they took their breakfast at the Café de l'Opéra, Clarissa's favorite place in the whole world. She was four and a half and had definite opinions about everything. Two days earlier, Taylor had taken her to a store called Printemps by himself. He was still trying to forge a bond with this wide-eyed bundle of energy.

Taylor and Allison had been married in the stone chapel of Iona. Brother Jonah had performed the ceremony. Ada Folley and Taylor's mother had flown over for the wedding, the first time either of them had ever been out of the country. Clarissa had carried the flowers down the aisle behind her mother, a cherubic expression of satisfaction on her face.

Clarissa would sit in his lap now and let him read to her. He could sit by her bed and hear her prayers. But he would catch her sometimes, staring at him in a very cautious way, as though uncertain who he truly was, or whether he would stay. These looks hurt him more than he could say. So Taylor took her shopping and bought her a new plaid dress and a bright red coat and a matching beret and wool mittens and tights and red patent leather shoes. Clarissa loved the color red. She loved how the salesladies spoke to her as they would a woman their own age. She loved how Taylor let her make all the choices herself. When they had returned from the shop and Clarissa had modeled her new outfit for her mother, Allison had rushed into the bathroom and sobbed so hard Taylor could hear her through the locked door.

They had the same breakfast every morning. Clarissa had a big pot of hot chocolate and her very own croissant. She tore off bites and dipped them into her oversized cup, just like she had seen the French people do, very careful not to drip anything on her new red outfit. Taylor went inside to use the café phone and called Guethary. When he returned to the table, Allison caught one glimpse of his face and said, "It's today?"

"They've booked me on the eleven o'clock express train."

"You need to hurry, then."

"Yes." Allison had asked not to go to the train station with him. He had agreed. His valise and the briefcase with all the legal documents were stationed between his chair and Allison's. He took his seat and reached for her hands. "I can't call you while I'm down there."

"We've been through all this." She squeezed his hand with both of hers. "It's going to be all right. Just miss me a little, all right?"

"Can I miss you a lot?"

Clarissa piped up from the table's other side, "Will you miss me too, Daddy?"

Taylor stared at her. She was a diminutive image of her

mother, the same huge eyes, the same hair somewhere between brown and blond, the same glowing skin. Only now she seemed to swim before his eyes. "What did you say?"

"I want you to miss me too."

Allison released one hand so as to cover her mouth. Taylor said very deliberately, "The only person I will miss more than you in the whole wide world is your mother."

"Where are you going?"

"To a village near some mountains south of here."

"Is it snowing there too?"

"Do you know, I forgot to ask. But I imagine that it is."

"How long will you be away?"

"I'm not certain. But I think three days." He added to Allison, "If it's any longer than that, I'll find some way to call you."

Clarissa observed her mother. "Mommy's sad because you're going away."

"I know. I'm sad too."

"But you're coming back, aren't you?"

Outside the window in front of their table, Paris was struggling beneath its winter burden. Traffic around the Place de l'Opéra was slow but steady. The day was gray, the trees bare, and the people bundled against the cold. But it was still Paris, and he was seated with two beautiful girls. Two people who cared for him and trusted him to be there for them.

Taylor rose from his chair, bent over, and kissed Allison. He then moved around so that two smaller arms could wrap around his neck. He said to them both, "Yes. I am coming back."

THE JOURNEY SOUTH WAS A TIME OF RECOLLECTION AND setting things in proper order. Taylor stared out the window as snow-covered lands whipped by at more than a hundred miles an hour. He was not touched by the speed, nor by the destination. What would come was beyond him. He had prepared as well as he could. He knew this now. He was trying his best to learn a new way of life. These changes of his went far beyond any physical act and touched at the eternal wellspring. He reached into his briefcase and withdrew the small traveling Bible he carried with him everywhere now. But he did not open it. The words in his head were clear enough. *Love never fails.*

Winter's gray remained in place through Bordeaux. When the train arrived in Biarritz, Taylor found he could not see the mountains at all. Inyakie greeted him with a solemn handshake and quiet words. They drove in easy silence into the mountains, following the Pilgrim's Route, the same one used by penitents for more than sixteen hundred years. The gray swept in until Taylor could see little more than the empty road ahead and the snowbanks to either side. Inyakie handled the car with the easy skill of one who would know the route blindfolded.

They overnighted in a hostel run by a local monastery. They were the only guests. The monks let them sleep in the central hall by the fire, the guesthouse's only source of heat.

The next morning a wind had strengthened, blowing in drier and warmer air from the southeast. Inyakie drove them further along the Compostelle Pass, then pulled down an unmarked side road and drove another two hours. When the road ended at the face of an ancient rock slide, they pulled packs from the trunk and headed off on foot.

The path was in truth not a path at all. They clambered over and around the snowy rock slide for almost an hour. Inyakie then led Taylor up a series of narrow steps, so crude they could only be identified by those who already knew the way.

They climbed and climbed and climbed, halting only once, for to stop meant to look down, and the drop was into looming emptiness. The steps curved gradually around the sheer cliff face until they were brought alongside a rushing, ice-encrusted river. Here the steps grew broader, and handholds were gouged from the rockface. Which was very good, as ice coated everything. Their progress became slower still.

When they reached what Taylor had expected would be the top, he discovered that they stood beside a semifrozen lake. The broad expanse was ringed on three sides by yet another curving cliff, this one seven hundred feet high. Over this cliff fell a semicircular waterfall. Winter's icy teeth dripped from every conceivable surface. Some of the lumpish daggers extended two hundred feet and more.

A narrow path traced around the lake's northern edge. With every spring thaw the path would disappear and not return until the next autumn's dry season. Inyakie unfurled a pair of waterproof ponchos from his backpack and handed one to Taylor. The path was partially covered by a natural depression in the cliff face. As they began clambering along the slick trail, a crack resounded from overhead. Inyakie shouted a warning. They plastered themselves to the stone wall as tons of ice rained down around them.

Spray from the waterfall was constant, filtering into his very bones. By the time they reached the lake's opposite end, Taylor was drenched and freezing.

Then Inyakie took a deep breath, gave Taylor a shivering grin, and disappeared beneath the falling water.

They entered a cave filled with the waterfall's thundering din. Inyakie withdrew a light from his pack and started forward.

They walked for almost an hour through the dank tunnel. With every step the temperature rose.

They emerged into an entirely new realm.

The bowl was less than a quarter of a mile wide. The cliff faces rose sheer on all sides. The sky overhead was now utterly blue, yet just an hour after noon the base was already in shadows. Taylor was not merely warm. He was *hot*. A series of boiling thermal springs turned the bowl into a high-altitude hothouse. He followed Inyakie's example and stripped down to shorts and T-shirt and hiking boots. Even so, by the time they descended to the forested base, he was sweating profusely.

Inyakie spoke for the first time since beginning the hike up the unmarked stairs. "Welcome to the true home of my father's oldest elixir, the *hyperclime.* To most this place remains nothing more than a legend. Those who know of this place, they call it the Basqueland's secret heart."

"I thank you for your confidence," Taylor replied.

Inyakie studied his feet a moment, then added, "Kirra is with child."

Taylor found himself nodding with his entire frame, as though any simpler motion would not have been enough. "Then this day is truly complete."

Jacques halted further talk by rounding the corner. He shook Taylor's hand and added his own careful inspection to Inyakie's.

Inyakie translated, "My father asks what progress you have made."

"He is not asking about our new corporation, is he?"

"Of course not."

Taylor chose his words with great care. "I don't know if I've learned enough yet even to answer. But I'm trying. And I'm praying. And I know that this learning will be a part of every day I have left on this earth."

Jacques had to reach up to take his grip upon Taylor's shoulders. This time he spoke in English, "Now I know that God's hand has been upon this since the beginning."

So it was that they took the path down to the campsite. To one side of the tents were stacked trays holding the precious plants, ready for Taylor to replant in his company's new hot-houses.

Then Kirra came into view, her form rounded by a future that did not contain him. And Taylor was able to greet her with a smile that truly came from the heart.

Revell Executive Ousted

THE BOARD OF PHARMACEUTICAL GIANT REVELL
Industries yesterday took the extraordinary step of firing its
CEO and largest shareholder, Amanda Revell, daughter of
founder Jack Revell.

Revell Industries, which has been losing market share over
the past three years, has become highly dependent on its Integrin
product. Widely prescribed for pain relief, Integrin was devel-
oped by Geneco Labs and acquired in a cash buyout by Revell
just prior to Integrin's release. Integrin is now reportedly

responsible for up to 75 percent of the Revell company's profit.

But Integrin's position as market leader has been challenged recently by Elixir Products, brainchild of former Revell employee Taylor Knox. Aided by Amanda Revell's own younger sister, a biochemist working on indigenous plant remedies in Europe, Knox has brought to market a natural therapy that competes directly with Integrin. This groundbreaking herbal remedy reportedly has no side effects. As reported in a *WSJ* feature last summer, interest in alternative medicine and traditional healing is on the rise. Knox's company is seen as a potential leader in this new wave.

Amanda Revell has recently been implicated in a corruption scandal involving the Food and Drug Administration. Two men who claim to have been in her direct employ have been convicted of offering bribes to government scientists to ban the Elixir line for health and safety reasons. Jackson Yerby, an American, and Colin Tomlinson, from Manchester in England, were both sentenced to seven years in prison by a federal court. They are said to be assisting the authorities in their investigation of Amanda Revell, who strenuously denies any link to these men.

For several months, there has been industry speculation about Knox bringing counterclaims against Revell. However, Knox is gaining a reputation for bringing his Christian values into the business world. This has earned him both scorn and praise in industry circles. Knox and his French partners have recently established a trust aimed at "preserving mankind's legacy of natural healing therapies."

When contacted by the *WSJ*, Knox confirmed that Amanda Revell had been directly involved in threatening both his life and livelihood. When asked what he intended to do about it, Knox was unequivocal. "Pray for her."

Look for Davis Bunn's
next suspense thriller

THE
LAZARUS
TRAP

Available Everywhere **Spring 2005**
From WestBow Press

WESTBOW
P R E S S
A Division of Thomas Nelson Publishers
Since 1798